Cody asked.

Lee summoned courage from somewhere. "I'd really rather not."

Slowly he moved his hands up her arms. "Why don't you relax and just be yourself?"

"This *is* myself."

He traced a finger along her face. "I don't think so."

Lee's breath caught in her lungs. It seemed to happen a lot around him.

Cody leaned toward her, her face framed in his hands. "I won't hurt you, Lee."

Yes, you will. The words echoed in her mind, but she left them unsaid. As his lips drew near, Lee still tried to tell herself she could handle this situation. She could handle anything.

No, she couldn't.

She knew it as soon as his lips touched hers. For now, for this one moment, she wouldn't think of what was to come. She would only think of now. And maybe, somehow, that would be enough....

Dear Reader,

Warning! Don't read April's terrific lineup of Silhouette Romance titles *unless* you're ready to catch spring fever!

The FABULOUS FATHERS series continues with Suzanne Carey's *Dad Galahad*. Ned Balfour, the story's hero, is all a modern knight should be—and *more*. Ned gallantly marries pregnant Jenny McClain to give her child a name. But he never expects the powerful emotions that come with being a father. *And* Jenny's husband.

Garrett Scott, the hero of *Who's That Baby?* by Kristin Morgan, is a father with a mysterious past. He's a man on the run, determined to protect his daughter. Then Garrett meets Whitney Arceneaux, a woman whose warmth and beauty tempt him to share his secret—and his heart.

Laurie Paige's popular ALL-AMERICAN SWEETHEARTS trilogy concludes this month with a passionate battle of wills in *Victoria's Conquest*. Jason Broderick fell in love with Victoria Broderick years ago—the day she married his late cousin. Now that Victoria is free and needs help, Jason will give her just about anything she wants. Anything *but* his love.

Rounding out the list, there's the sparkling, romantic mix-up of Patricia Ellis's *Sorry, Wrong Number* and Maris Soule's delightful and moving love story, *Lyon's Pride*. One of your favorite authors, Marie Ferrarella blends just the right touch of heartfelt emotion, warmth and humor in *The Right Man*.

In the coming months, look for more books by your favorite authors, including Diana Palmer, Elizabeth August, Phyllis Halldorson and many more.

Happy reading from all of us at Silhouette!

Anne Canadeo
Senior Editor

THE RIGHT MAN
Marie Ferrarella

Silhouette
R O M A N C E™
Published by Silhouette Books New York
America's Publisher of Contemporary Romance

To Valerie Hayward
In friendship

SILHOUETTE BOOKS
300 E. 42nd St., New York, N.Y. 10017

THE RIGHT MAN

Copyright © 1993 by Marie Rydzynski-Ferrarella

All rights reserved. Except for use in any review, the reproduction or utilization of this work in whole or in part in any form by any electronic, mechanical or other means, now known or hereafter invented, including xerography, photocopying and recording, or in any information storage or retrieval system, is forbidden without the permission of the publisher, Silhouette Books, 300 E. 42nd St., New York, N.Y. 10017

ISBN: 0-373-08932-5

First Silhouette Books printing April 1993

All the characters in this book have no existence outside the imagination of the author and have no relation whatsoever to anyone bearing the same name or names. They are not even distantly inspired by any individual known or unknown to the author, and all incidents are pure invention.

®: Trademark used under license and registered in the United States Patent and Trademark Office and in other countries.

Printed in the U.S.A.

Books by Marie Ferrarella

Silhouette Romance

The Gift #588
Five-Alarm Affair #613
Heart to Heart #632
Mother for Hire #686
Borrowed Baby #730
Her Special Angel #744
*The Undoing of
   Justin Starbuck* #766
Man Trouble #815
The Taming of the Teen #839
Father Goose #869
Babies on His Mind #920
The Right Man #932

Silhouette Special Edition

It Happened One Night #597
A Girl's Best Friend #652
Blessing in Disguise #675
Someone To Talk To #703
World's Greatest Dad #767

Silhouette Books

Silhouette Christmas Stories 1992
"The Night Santa Claus Returned"

Books by Marie Ferrarella writing as Marie Nicole

Silhouette Romance

Man Undercover #373
Please Stand By #394
Mine by Write #411
Getting Physical #440

Silhouette Desire

Tried and True #112
Buyer Beware #142
Through Laughter and Tears #161
Grand Theft: Heart #182
A Woman of Integrity #197
Country Blue #224
Last Year's Hunk #274
Foxy Lady #315
Chocolate Dreams #346
No Laughing Matter #382

MARIE FERRARELLA

was born in Europe, raised in New York City, and now lives in Southern California. She describes herself as the tired mother of two overenergetic children and the contented wife of one wonderful man. She is thrilled to be following her dream of writing full-time.

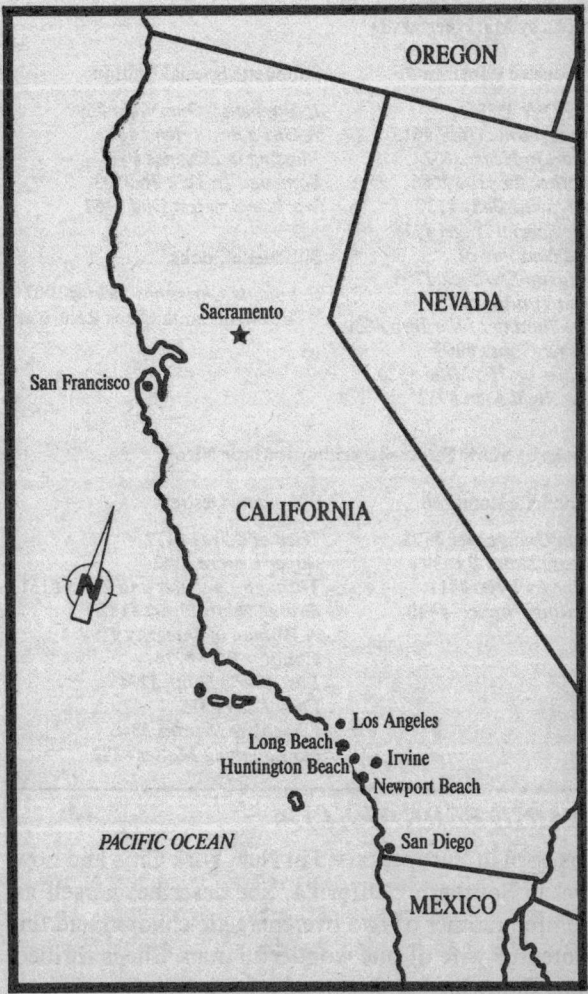

Chapter One

Her eyes opened slowly. Half a minute later, her mind kicked in. It was time to get up. She was awake, or at least conscious, which at this hour was the best she could hope for.

She stirred, part of her still trying desperately to hang on to sleep.

The immediate world around her was surrounded in a dark, misty shroud. How could it be time to wake up so soon? She'd just closed her eyes two minutes ago. Okay, maybe three, she amended.

Leanne Sheridan sighed and reluctantly sat up as she dragged one hand through her tangled blond hair. Last night she had closed the curtains around her canopy bed. The effect had comforted her. Being surrounded in a light blue haze created a dreamy atmosphere. And last night she had wanted to dream pleasant, peaceful dreams.

She sat there for a minute, trying to collect her thoughts before she started pushing the curtain away from her bed in a poor imitation of the breaststroke until she found an opening. She leaned over, reaching for the clock on her nightstand. Her fingers quickly groped for the switch on top of the clock and found it just in time to prevent the tooth-grating alarm from shattering the predawn air. She had a habit of waking up moments before her alarm clock went off.

Undoubtedly a habit born of self-preservation, she thought vaguely, wishing with all her heart that today was Saturday instead of Friday.

Lee stared at the glaring red numbers. It took a moment for them to register, even though she knew what they were supposed to read. Six o'clock. The groan that echoed in the room escaped her lips under its own volition.

"God doesn't even get up until six-thirty," she mumbled.

She stretched her athletic frame to its limit, then relaxed. Exhausted and hoping for anything that would permit her to spend the morning in bed, she lingered a few more seconds. Her eyes started to drift shut when the dark, hairy lump at the foot of the bed shifted slightly, crushing her toes.

"All right, Pussycat, I'm up, I'm up. Satisfied? Up and at 'em, right?"

A regal head rose, transforming the furry lump at her feet into a malamute. The dog eyed her for a long minute before yawning and lowering his head on top of his paws.

Lee leaned forward and scratched Pussycat's head. She smiled fondly. "I don't blame you. Matter of fact, right now I wish I *were* you." She focused her attention on what lay ahead of her. An entire day, starting with a rude separation from her bed. Not only that, but today was the day *he* came in, the dreaded new general production manager. Who knew what the end of the day would bring?

She tumbled out of bed, the sheet still clinging to her waist. It took a couple of minutes to disentangle herself. She was not one of those people who slept as if she were dead. She slept, her mother had once observed, like a windup toy moving from one corner of the bed to the other and generally wrecking havoc on the bedding as she went.

Lee sighed. "There must be a better way to pay bills."

If there was a better way to earn a living, she hadn't found it. She loved her work doing voice characterizations at Hayward Studios. Variations of her voice were heard coming out of the mouths of some of the most popular cartoon characters on television.

She reached the end of the plush gray throw rug and came in contact with the wooden floor. Her toes curled reflexively. It was an unusually cold, wet autumn and all the dampness seemed to be seeping into her floor. Into her house, she amended as she moved through the unlit bedroom toward the bathroom. The chill and gloom outside wouldn't burn off until ten in the morning. Just in time for first break at the studio.

She had been involved in doing voice characterizations for over five years, first at one studio and then another before she found her niche at Hayward three years ago. It was worth absolutely everything she had to go through, even though she was hard-pressed to admit it at this hour. Later, when the joy exploded within her, when the self-satisfaction had a chance to take hold as it did every morning by the time she faced the microphone, she'd look back and feel that getting up at six was a small sacrifice to pay for all this.

But at this moment in time, as her body yearned for five more minutes in bed, it was difficult working up her enthusiasm.

Lee switched on the light in her baby-blue bathroom with its Victorian fixtures and blinked at the image that stared back at her in the mirror.

Her hair was disheveled. Her eyes were still half-shut, and her face looked as if someone had slept on it. Actually, someone had. Lee had never broken herself of the habit of sleeping on her stomach and burying her head in her pillow. Her cheeks bore creases from her satin pillowcase.

Lee tossed her long hair back over her shoulder, put her hands on her hips and gazed intently at the reflection. "Hello, Gorgeous." Barbra Streisand's voice suddenly occupied the same area as she did.

She had started out doing voice impersonations to entertain her friends at school. Eventually, that had led to her present profession. And food on her table.

Reluctantly, she moved toward the shower stall, then shed the oversize jersey she slept in, letting it fall to the tiled floor. "Well, no time like the present." She opened the shower door. With a flick of her wrist, she turned the water on. Icy needles sprayed out. Lee shivered involuntarily.

She stepped in to face her torture, biting her lower lip to refrain from uttering a few well-chosen curses.

She showered and dressed in half an hour rather than twenty minutes. The extra ten minutes had her running behind schedule. She debated skipping breakfast, then rejected the idea. She had to have breakfast. If she neglected her stomach, it would avenge itself when she least expected it, ruining a taping session.

All she had time for was a slice of toast. She washed it down with coffee that was strong enough to do bench presses on its own, thanks to her malfunctioning coffeemaker. As she ate on the move, Pussycat followed her around the kitchen.

"No, I'm not going to forget about you, Pussycat. Not to worry." She rummaged through the refrigerator until she found the container of sweet-and-sour chicken she had picked up last night. "How's this?" She held up the would-be feast. Pussycat danced back and forth in agitated anticipation.

"Are you sure you're not half-human?" she asked as she dumped the contents of the white box into the dog dish. Pussycat nudged her out of the way and attacked his food as if he hadn't eaten in weeks.

Lee sat back on her heels, watching the dog she had nursed back to health after finding him on her doorstep late one night. He bore no resemblance to that animal any longer. Tender loving care, that was what had done the trick, she thought as she rose to her feet. That and food. Too bad people didn't respond to it the way animals did.

Involuntarily, she thought of Lloyd. The quick flash of memory made her shiver, the way she always did when she thought of Lloyd and their life together. But that was history, and her mind should be on the future. She refused to let memories return to haunt her. They were for nightmares.

"Be good," she warned the dog and then left.

The top of her Volkswagen Cabriolet was stuck in the down position and would probably stay that way until she could find the time to see her mechanic. In deference to the early morning mist that hung over Southern California like a veil, Lee had stuffed her thick, wavy blond hair under a black fedora that had once belonged to her father.

She caught a glimpse of herself in the rearview mirror that was knocked sideways again. She straightened it so that she could get a clear view of the headlights behind her. "I look like a gun moll." She laughed, liking the image. "Wonder if Mr. Cody What's-his-name likes gun molls."

She was nervous and she knew it. Her hands kept sliding down the steering wheel. A new general production manager could mean a new position—on the unemployment line. The studio was in the red and had been for two years now. The new man had been brought in to make the necessary cutbacks in order to get Hayward Studios financially back on its feet. With one stroke of the pen, the cartoons she worked on could become only a vague memory on some obscure cable station, trapped in endless reruns.

Lee murmured a prayer as she drove.

The studio parking lot was already half-full by the time she drove up. Small, economical, the entire studio complex was nestled on a little more than half an acre of land. Three-quarters of it was devoted to the animation department, the remainder to the soundtrack recording section. Begun in the thirties, the studio had a proud history of, not to mention numerous awards for, cartoon excellence. When limited animation had come in, the studio head had stuck by his guns and refused to allow the quality of Hayward Cartoons to deteriorate. It was an expensive decision. And therein lay the beginning of the problem.

She hoped that somehow the new man Caleb Hayward had brought in could work a miracle or two and turn the situation around without sacrificing any of the shows she and her friends worked on. The people she worked with were closer to her than her own family was, and she would have hated to see any of them let go. Taking a deep breath, she parked her car between a blue Mustang and a car that had once been a Nissan but was now a hybrid of several automobiles by virtue of welded-on parts. It belonged to Elyse Duncan, the chief sound engineer.

Lee pushed open the heavy glass front door and walked down the dimly lit hallway, her high-heeled sandals clicking on the linoleum. She tugged off her hat, and her hair tumbled down. Raking one hand through it carelessly, she let it fall where it wanted to. She could feel the energy charging up in her veins. It happened every time she walked into the studio. There was something about the small, dusky hallway, the musky odor of the floor polish that the cleaning lady applied once a week, that always got to her.

Face it, she thought, *you're hopelessly hooked on floor polish.*

"Good morning, Elyse!" she called out as she walked onto the soundstage. She nodded at several technicians in the area, then turned toward Elyse. She was immediately struck by the older woman's clothes. In place of her customary jeans, Elyse was wearing a dress.

Lee widened her eyes and placed her hand on her heart. "Elyse, you have legs!"

Elyse narrowed her eyes as she turned to look at Lee. "Of course I have legs."

Lee shrugged innocently. "I've been here three years and I've never seen them." She tucked her hands into the back pockets of her jeans. "New studio rule?"

Elyse wrinkled up her nose. Freckles met freckles. "Just trying to create a favorable first impression." She looked Lee's five-foot-three frame over critically. "It wouldn't have hurt you any to dress up."

Lee clutched at her heart again. "Oh, the pain, the pain."

"Comedian." Elyse frowned.

Lee's grin hid the jumble of nerves inside. "A good sense of humor never hurts."

She looked in the direction of the glass enclosure and saw the director for the "Sammy and Shadoe Show" in conference with one of the story editors. Were they discussing this week's show, or deciding how to best update their résumés?

"So, when's the big man coming?" Lee asked, turning to Elyse.

Elyse was looking over her notes about the sounds needed for the day's work and was momentarily distracted. Lee's question barely registered. "Who?"

"Santa Claus," Lee quipped. "Who do you think? Cody What's-his-name."

"Lancaster," Elyse supplied.

Lee nodded. Why had she forgotten it? It was such a simple name. "As in Burt."

"As in our future," Elyse reminded her needlessly.

"No pressure, right?" Lee struggled to keep her anxiety under wraps. "So, when does our future get here?" And how long before these butterflies settle down? she added silently.

"He's supposed to be here around nine. I hear he wants to hold two big general meetings, one with the animation department, one with the sound people."

"Oh-oh."

Elyse's face reflected the concern they all felt. "Maybe he just wants to introduce himself."

Without thinking, Lee flipped through Elyse's notes, not seeing them. "And maybe he wants to tell us which one of us is getting the ax."

Elyse carefully took back her notes. "Hey, where's that natural optimism of yours?"

It wasn't natural. She had to work at it all the time. But that had been Lloyd's fault, something Elyse knew nothing about. No one at the studio did. "It's on vacation." She turned to leave Elyse's booth.

"Hey, Lee," Elyse called after her.

Lee turned, one hand on the doorknob. "Yes?"

"They say he's cute."

She shrugged. "Just as long as he doesn't mess with any of my shows, he can be positively adorable." She saw the look in Elyse's eyes. "And I make you a present of him."

"I wish."

Lee laughed as she closed the door behind her and entered a land of fantasy, at least for the next two hours.

The radio in Cody Lancaster's sleek Jaguar was set to a radio station he had discovered his second day in Southern California. They played only oldies. It brought back memories. Maybe too many. But for the time being, he'd settle for that. That and work.

He liked work, and right now work was a very necessary commodity to him. If he immersed himself in it, maybe it could help him ease the pain. The only thing he wanted to have time for was restoring a sense of routine for himself and for Sean.

He smiled when he thought of his five-year-old son. Sean was the reason he had stayed sane these last thirteen months after Deborah had died and his life fell apart. Sean meant the world to Cody.

His mother's death had caused Sean to recede into himself. These days, Cody's towheaded little boy wasn't a boy anymore. He was any one of a number of animals. Cody's sister, Sara, had promised that it was just a phase that Sean would outgrow. Cody liked to think that she was right, but even though she was the mother of four, he still had his doubts about the situation. There were times when he felt he should be doing something, anything, to help, but what? He hated just letting things slide, but he had absolutely no idea what he could do.

Love and patience, Sara had said. Somehow, it didn't seem enough.

"I started out with a baby boy and wound up with a pet," Cody muttered to himself.

He braked as a red sports car cut him off. A wandering mind, he told himself, was not advisable on the freeway. He had thought that driving was rough in the heart of the city, but New York traffic came in second when it was pitted against the elaborate maze found here in California. He couldn't shake the feeling that he should be donning a helmet.

A knight about to do battle. It kind of fit the idea he had about coming to work for Hayward Studios. He had done a lot of background research and checking before he had agreed to take on this job. His last position had been a rather tame job at a studio in New York. They produced daytime dramas, quite a differ-

ent thing from handling the business end of philosophical squirrels and colorful lands of enchantment that
were created to make children smile. And yield a healthy
corporate profit.

He had a feeling that what lay ahead of him was a
definite challenge, and right now it was just what he
needed, what he wanted. He had given New York a year
before deciding that it wasn't working. He and Sean
needed a change of scene, a chance to start over again,
fresh, in a city where they weren't constantly reminded
of Deborah and the loss they both shared. So, he had
taken a job across the country.

It had occurred to Cody, too late, that possibly a
stretch of time back home in Dallas would have done
them both some good.

Maybe he and Sean would go back for a visit by
Christmas.

The room was filled with people, some sitting, most
standing. He had called the meeting only to introduce
himself and to let them know that no changes were going to be made without first carefully considering all
angles. He didn't want to go in, slashing shows aimlessly. If productions were eventually scrapped, then
possibly the people involved could be utilized else-
where. The bottom line for the time being was that no
one was being let go immediately and never without
warning.

That was what he had intended to say. And he had
gotten most of it out, but his thoughts became slightly
muddled right after he noticed her. She stood against
the doorjamb, watching him. From the first moment he
saw her, she struck him as an intriguing puzzle. Her
aquamarine eyes smoldered with a pixieish humor that

he found difficult to tie in with the sensuous woman who stood leaning against the door, watching him nonchalantly. Her arms were crossed before her chest, almost covering the T-shirt that proclaimed: They can't fire me, slaves have to be sold.

He wondered who she was and if she was going to be trouble. If so, trouble had never come wrapped in a more intriguing package.

Cody was surprised by his reaction to her, and pleased in a way. He had had what he thought to be the perfect marriage with Deborah. They had shared ten wonderful years together, and when she had died so suddenly from pneumonia, he had felt as if his world, his very life, had ended. Loving Sean had sustained him, but as far as looking at other women, it was as if something within him had been short-circuited or had malfunctioned. He wasn't interested in seeing anyone or having another relationship, ever.

In a way it was a relief to find out that he wasn't dead anymore, though part of him was surprised and almost saddened by the knowledge.

He was looking at her. Was he just making eye contact, or was there some hidden message being transmitted that she was missing? Lee wondered. Should she be trying to remember the address of the unemployment office? Lee felt her pulse quicken, and it wasn't because he was even more handsome than Elyse had indicated. He was, she thought, remembering a phrase she had once read, "a thinking woman's hunk." Except that this woman was thinking in terms of survival.

Could she survive him?

He sounded sincere, but that wouldn't stop him from making major cuts if it was necessary. She knew she could always look for work at another studio, but it was never easy, and this had become home to her. That was important to Lee—belonging, on however small a scale.

Her palms began to sweat. Casually, she uncrossed her arms and pressed her hands against her thighs in order to blot the wetness from them.

Her thighs became damp. Terrific.

Cody was trying to maintain eye contact with each of the people assembled in his office, but his eyes kept drifting back toward hers. There was something there, something compelling that beckoned to him.

Did she know it? he wondered. Did she know the kind of signals she was sending out? Who was she? He made a mental note to pull out her file from the myriad of personnel folders he had had his new secretary bring in.

Cody refocused his attention. He was talking, yet thinking of something else. He hoped he hadn't been babbling incoherently. It was time to wrap it up. He didn't want to bore them to death at their first meeting.

"Well, that's about it, except that I look forward to speaking to each of you by the end of this week or the next at the very latest. I want to be a hands-on production manager."

Elyse leaned toward Lee and whispered, "He can have his hands on me anytime."

Lee didn't answer. People around them were beginning to leave. She turned, ready to go with the tide. Out of the corner of her eye, she saw that Cody was still watching her.

When he saw that he had caught her attention, Cody made an impulsive decision. "Miss?"

Lee hoped her voice wouldn't crack, especially not with everyone looking at them. "Yes?"

"I'd like to start with you." For some reason, his voice sounded half an octave lower. Authoritative, but definitely sexy. Did general managers sound sexy just before they fired you? Lee felt her throat go dry as she took a step closer toward Cody.

"Lucky you," Elyse murmured as she passed Lee on her way out.

Lee didn't feel lucky. He was going to fire her. She couldn't think of any other reason for being singled out. He was going to fire her, no matter what words he had said to the contrary. But if she was going, she was going to go out in style, she told herself.

Lee put one hand on her hip, pushed out her lower lip and Mae West murmured, "Start what with me?"

Some people around her laughed as they left the office, but her eyes were only on Cody. He looked bemused.

The man has no sense of humor and I'm a dead, unemployed duck.

Everyone filed out, leaving her alone with Cody. The man was tall, blond, athletic, classically featured and looked like an ad for a shirt commercial. She felt utterly defenseless. Lee watched as he walked around his neat desk which was covered with nicely squared folders and papers, and took a seat.

Neat. The man has a neat desk. I never trust a man with a neat desk. There's something not quite human about being able to keep track of everything.

Cody gestured toward the chair in front of his desk. Lee was barely conscious of lowering herself into it.

"Do I get a blindfold?"

He narrowed his eyes beneath finely arched wheat-colored eyebrows. "Excuse me?"

She waved her hand in the air in a large circle. "Before I face the firing squad—pardon the pun."

Surprise registered as he tried to uncover what she was talking about. "You think I'm going to fire you?"

"You think you're not?" she quipped back.

He shook his head as if to clear it. It didn't help. "I'm going to need a minute to sort that one out."

"Take all the time you need." She glanced at her wristwatch. "I don't have to be anywhere for the next nine minutes." *Provided I have a show to do.*

He leaned back in his chair as he looked at her. "Nine minutes?"

"That's when we're supposed to start taping again. Unless you have other ideas."

"My first idea is that I'd like to know your name."

Oh God, here it comes. Maybe he's just doing this at random. "Leanne Sheridan."

Cody spread out some of the files on his desk, looking for hers. The silence was awful. She could have heard herself drawing breath—if she had been breathing.

"Ah, here it is."

Her stomach tightened, then flip-flopped. She folded her hands in front of it and offered a grin she didn't feel. "Does the FBI know that's missing?"

He thumbed through the manila folder, scanning the pages quickly. Her list of credits was extensive. "Impressive." He put the folder down again. "You work on a lot of our shows."

She raised her chin proudly. It was a slight movement that he found stirring. "I eat a good breakfast every morning. It gives me extra energy."

Cody stared at her, then began to laugh. He hadn't really laughed since before Deborah had died. Silently, he thanked Lee for the moment.

Lee watched him, wondering if he was really laughing, or if he was trying to put her at ease as he came in for the kill.

Chapter Two

Lee shifted uncomfortably in the large brown leather chair. The sound of Cody's laughter had died away, and he seemed to be studying her intently. If she were at a party right now, Lee would have guessed that she was being assessed as to her receptive possibilities. In response to his long, sweeping look, she would have said something flippant and walked away. But Cody's appraisal was different. She couldn't quite put her finger on it, but somehow, it was just different. Serious. And sad in a way.

Why?

Oh, stop it, she thought. *You're reading too much into it. He's probably wondering if you're worth the money the studio's paying you.*

She felt antsy. She'd never been the type to simply wait out a situation. She had to have things resolved. Now. Unconsciously searching for support, she gripped the arms of the chair. "Are there any other questions you'd like to ask me?"

For the first time in years, Cody found himself actually looking at a woman, really looking at her. There was something about Leanne that demanded that sort of attention. She wasn't exactly beautiful. But there was something more, something that left a lasting impression rather than evoked a fleeting response. She was captivating, vibrant. Alive. Mischievous. And, she seemed to be managing it all at once.

"Yes," he answered, then added silently, *yes I'd like to get to know you better.* The thought surprised him as much as the verbalization of the sentence would have surprised her.

Lee waited. The single word wasn't being followed by any others. She was growing increasingly uneasy. Maybe he didn't like firing people, or couldn't find the right phrases. That was fine with her. If he didn't find the words, maybe he wouldn't act on them.

There were a lot of questions that suddenly posed themselves to Cody. Questions that had nothing to do with work.

He didn't know what came over him. Maybe it was just part of the mourning/healing process. Maybe his male hormones were waking up after hibernation and, like a bear, they were phenomenally hungry. Cody had not felt even so much as a passing interest in another woman since he had married Deborah. And after her death, it was as if he had been burned out inside, as if his ability to love, to seek a male-female relationship had been completely taken away from him, had been buried with Deborah.

Having accepted that, Cody would have been satisfied to go on thinking that was the way things were meant to be. To find out that they weren't, that he could feel a purely male reaction when in the company of an intriguing woman, was a little shattering.

And encouraging.

Cody felt definitely confused.

Maybe he had been too quick to uproot himself and Sean. Maybe he should have stayed back in New York City, working at the studio there until he had straightened the emotional turmoil that Deborah's death and Sean's descent into the animal kingdom had put his life into.

Too late now, buddy, he told himself. *You're here.*

She wasn't doing well under his scrutiny. Though her mind was on her job, she felt a reaction that had little to do with work. She felt warm. Stirred. And she was losing her composure, fast. Maybe it was just her imagination. Either that, or the thermostat had gone berserk again.

Lee had felt a great deal more comfortable around the old general production manager, John Makepeace, with his pot belly, his toupee and his indecision. He had let the studio more or less run itself, which was why he'd been replaced. He hadn't posed a threat of any kind. And there was something very threatening about Cody Lancaster, something beyond the realm of salaries.

She cleared her throat. Time to get the show on the road. "Does this interview—"

"Meeting," he corrected.

She inclined her head, conceding the point. Cody had a feeling that she didn't do that very often. "Meeting. Does it come in installments?"

Cody raised his brows, trying to discern the gist of her question. It would have helped a lot if they spoke the same language, he thought. He was very partial to

English and almost said so. "Would you like to re-phrase that, please?"

She wished she could relax. The tension gripping her was beginning to wear her out. Lee took a deep breath before going on. Her voice, when she spoke again, was at least an octave lower than normal. It happened when she was nervous. Her life was finally going just the way she wanted it to. She loved her job at the studio, long hours, hectic pace and all. And one word from Cody could ruin everything.

"Well, those nine minutes that you—" she stopped herself, regrouping "—that *we* had are now down to three." She licked her lips. They felt incredibly dry. "The director isn't going to be happy with me if I hold up production."

Unconsciously, he followed the path of her tongue as it darted along the outline of her mouth and felt himself responding. Boy, when those hormones let loose, they really let loose, he thought sarcastically, annoyed with himself. "That's very conscientious of you."

Lee couldn't decide if he was commending her or being subtly sarcastic. How was she going to play this? Life certainly wasn't easy this morning. Where was that pudding-faced John Makepeace when she needed him? Lee straightened in her seat, still holding on to the armrests.

Cody wondered how long it would take her to rip the arms off the chair.

"I'm a very conscientious sort of a person, in my own way." Lee was beginning to feel as if some sort of a different game was being played out on another level, a game whose rules she hadn't been given yet. "And I like my job. We all do," she added quickly, putting in a plug for the crew at large.

"That's good to know." Cody leaned back in his chair. If pressed, he wouldn't have been able to accurately explain why he was enjoying this conversation. He just knew he was. Maybe that was enough. For now.

There had been concrete things that he had planned to ask her, things about her career goals, how she viewed her position at the studio. If she had any input about the way things were handled. But he had gotten sidetracked by a quirky smile and the incredible amount of nervous energy that was being generated before him. It was time to retreat before things drifted any further. Cody sought for something to say now that would keep him from appearing totally incompetent.

"I'm just trying to get a better handle on the people who work at the studio."

Was that all? She felt a huge sense of relief as she flashed a wide, easy smile. "I'm not a tote bag, Mr. Lancaster. I don't come with handles. Or labels."

"I'm beginning to see that."

Though she couldn't have said why, Lee felt on safer ground now than she did a minute ago. Time to wind this up. "Are you going to cancel 'Sammy and Shadoe'?"

She was direct in an offbeat sort of way. He liked that. "I'm not cancelling anything yet. First I just want to observe and make assessments."

"That sounds hopeful." *For now.* Lee rose, and as she extended her hand, she said in a high-pitched voice that children would immediately recognize as belonging to Sammy Squirrel, "They're waiting for me to give them five pages of dialogue right now, or I'll have to give up my winter's supply of nuts."

Cody's brows narrowed as he searched his memory. The voice she was using was vaguely familiar, but its identity eluded him.

She liked the way surprise highlighted his features. It made him look softer, maybe a little less smolderingly sexy. No, she amended, the only thing that would make Cody Lancaster look less sexy would be a paper bag over his head. Maybe his whole body. And even then it was a qualified maybe.

Lee shook her head slightly, as if that would clear it. Elyse's earlier comments about Cody's raw male looks must have burrowed themselves into her brain and were now acting like a post-hypnotic suggestion. Otherwise, there'd be no reason for her to be reacting this way.

No reason except for twenty-twenty vision, she thought.

"You sound just like—like—" Cody snapped his fingers repeatedly, looking for the name that refused to materialize for him.

"Sammy Squirrel," Lee supplied. "Are you a fan?" She fluttered her eyelashes at him. "I'm flattered."

Mischief looked good on her, he thought. "Not me, my five-year-old son, Sean."

Something small and nameless sank in the pit of her stomach. Son. Family. Wife. He was married. Aren't the best ones always taken?

There are no best ones, she reminded herself. *You learned that the hard way.*

Refocusing her mind, she told herself that all she cared about was keeping her cast of characters alive at the studio. Lee grinned at Cody, perhaps a little too widely. "Bring him around sometime and I'll make squirrel noises for him."

Cody laughed. Lee could have sworn she heard a tinge of frustration in his laugh. "He might make noises right back at you."

"Does he like to mimic?" She thought back to her own childhood and the hours spent in front of the television, pretending to be everyone she saw on the screen. Pretending so that she wouldn't have to hear the sound of raised, angry voices or doors being slammed. "I can relate to that."

"No, Sean doesn't mimic. He just thinks he's an animal, or so he says." The words came out naturally, without thought. He realized he was talking to her as if she was an old friend, as if he had known her a long time instead of just a few minutes. There was something about her face, about her manner, that encouraged him to open up. Or maybe things had just been bottled up inside him too long. At any rate, he heard himself telling her something he hadn't even told his own parents. Only his sister.

Lee smiled wider, and Cody found himself responding again. "I know a lot of kids who act like animals."

"No, not act. Is."

Lee stared at him. "Excuse me?"

He shouldn't have started this. Cody broke eye contact and began to straighten the folders on his desk. "Sean really thinks he's an animal."

"Oh." Suddenly, Lee wasn't making small talk to her new boss any longer. She had taken a quantum leap into the realm of friend and was mulling over his problem. It took no more than that for her. She was quick to befriend. There was only one line she wouldn't cross, couldn't cross no matter how much she wanted what laid on the other side.

Automatically, Lee reached out and touched Cody's shoulder. "Don't worry, he'll outgrow it."

Cody looked into her eyes. A man could drown in aquamarine eyes like that. Cody forced himself to put distance between his words and his thoughts. "So they tell me."

Lee dropped her hand. "Well, I've got to dash."

She didn't have to look over her shoulder to know that he was watching her as she left. She had a feeling that a lot remained unsaid between them.

And it would stay that way if she had anything to do with it.

Elyse pounced on her as soon as she walked back into the soundstage. "Well, what did he say? What did he want? What's he *really* like?" Elyse breathed.

"He wants my body. He started breathing heavy right after everyone left, and we're naming our first child after you." Lee laughed at Elyse's reaction. "Put your eyes back in your head, Elyse. You look like a dead ringer for Little Orphan Annie."

Elyse waved an annoyed hand at Lee, her fingers a blur of scarlet. "Why can't you ever be serious?"

"Because it's no fun." Lee had lowered her voice and assumed the hushed tones of a popular cartoon villainess with a Transylvanian lisp. She looked around, then inclined her head toward the room she had just left. "Don't vorry, your time vill come."

Elyse looked confused, which was not an unusual state around Lee.

"He said he wanted to talk to everyone, remember?" Lee said in her own voice.

The smile on Elyse's face threatened to slide up to her earring-laced ears. "Yes, he did."

"Now, if there are no further questions—" Lee turned on her heel "—I think our beloved director would rather that we got on with it."

"Very perceptive of you, Lee," the bald-headed man said as he motioned Lee out of the sound booth, pointing to the microphone in the middle of the room. Two other cast members were already assembled there. "Unless, of course, you'd like to take up a different line of work."

"Not me, I'm happy as a lark here." She chirped for his benefit as she passed him. The two men at the microphone laughed.

She had gotten involved in doing different voice characterizations professionally five years ago. Initially, she had taken the job in order to keep herself fed and busy, as if earning a degree in communications from UCI wasn't time-consuming enough. But she hadn't wanted any time to think, to dwell on the wrong turns her life had taken in such a short time. It had taken her six months to pull her life together after she finally divorced Lloyd and twice that long to rebuild her battered self-esteem. Working at the studio helped enormously. And somewhere along the line, she had gotten hooked. A couple of the characters she did, Princess Enchantra, ruler of Zanadu, and Sammy Squirrel, the brainy half of Sammy and Shadoe, had endured year after year in the killer market field of Saturday morning cartoons.

And hopefully, she thought, picking up her script, they would continue to endure.

Cody seemed to be everywhere the first week, watching, jotting down notes, and succeeding in making everyone incredibly nervous. It seemed to Lee that every time she looked up, Cody was somewhere in the immediate vicinity, observing. At times there was a strange expression on his face, an expression she couldn't fathom.

She thought about the past week as she and Elyse got ready to leave the studio. The weekend was ahead of her, but she knew she was going to have no peace until she found out for certain that neither she nor any of the programs she loved were going to be scrapped. The 'Sammy and Shadoe Show' was the most costly to produce of the Hayward Studio lineup. But also, if she were to believe the ratings, it was the most popular show. Still, stranger things had happened than having a popular program pulled. And it was, after all, just a cartoon. The fate of the free world did not depend on it. But it was her program, and her favorite one at that.

"What do you suppose he's up to?" she asked Elyse.

"Nothing much with me, but he seems to have his eyes on you." There was no mistaking the wistful envy in Elyse's voice.

For once, Lee didn't feel like trading quips. "I know. That's what has me worried. Why me?"

"Maybe he just likes to look. You aren't exactly repulsive, you know," Elyse pointed out.

Lee was certain that wasn't it. "If the man wanted to ogle, he has only to walk in any direction and find himself on a beach where the women are wearing less and less and the men are leering more and more."

Elyse shrugged. "Maybe he doesn't like sand."

"Then he picked the wrong state to live in." Lee slid her arms into her denim jacket and picked up her purse from the floor next to Elyse's desk where she had dropped it. "I don't know, Elyse. He makes me uneasy."

"Yeah, me, too." The woman sighed.

"Not that way." She saw Elyse's skeptical look as they headed out the door. "Okay, okay, maybe that way too, just a little." Maybe more than just a little, she admitted silently, but that was only for her to know. "But I mean about my job. I liked having Makepeace around much better. He just sat in his office and smoked cigars."

"Which is why he's doing it at the unemployment office these days," Elyse informed her.

Lee stopped, concerned. "You mean, he really can't find another job—?"

Elyse stopped Lee before she could get going. "Hold it. Before you start talking about doing a fund-raiser for the man, I was only kidding. Makepeace is married to money, remember? He doesn't have to do anything but smoke cigars for the rest of his life if he doesn't want to." A freckled hand encompassed the area to emphasize her point. "This was more like a hobby to him, which is why the studio's in trouble these days."

Elyse looked at Lee and shook her head, her tightly curled red hair bouncing around her face. "Honestly, Lee, you'd think at your age you would have hardened up a little."

"The day I harden up, Elyse, is the day I die. See you."

Cody stood just out of sight of Elyse's booth. He hadn't meant to eavesdrop. He'd been on his way to see Elyse to discuss a few of the cuts he had come up with that involved the sound people. He had wanted to do it himself, not believing in delegating sensitive matters. But he had gotten intrigued by the conversation before he could make his presence known. And more intrigued by the woman who espoused so many causes.

He had already read in her folder that whenever the studio got involved in a charity event, like the upcoming one this Saturday, she was first in line to volunteer her services. He couldn't help wondering what it was that drove her. He also couldn't help noticing that she was occupying his thoughts more and more. He was going to have to do something about that.

Cody didn't really know what made him hustle Sean into his Jaguar early the next morning and drive to Irvine's UCI campus. It wasn't as if he cared about baseball. He wasn't sports oriented. But the studio was cosponsoring a fund-raiser that was being held in the large field just beyond Crawford Hall. Baseball celebrities from bygone years were playing against one another in an all-time all-star game. The proceeds were to go to help house the homeless. Lee had volunteered to help emcee the competition.

"This is part of Dad's new job," Cody was saying to Sean, or perhaps more to himself, as they drove down from Huntington Beach. He reasoned that it would do him good to see some of the studio employees on an informal basis. He was shadowboxing and he knew it, but he wasn't quite ready to tell himself the real reason he was going.

Sean sat next to him, sullen, staring out the window. Cody knew that he had drawn his son away from his main source of entertainment. But the VCR was taking care of that little detail for them.

"Sammy Squirrel will still be there for you when we get back," Cody assured Sean.

Large green eyes that reminded him so much of Deborah looked up at Cody, a silent accusation shining there.

Cody strove to find patience. "Listen, when I was a kid, we didn't have VCRs to catch what we missed. If we missed it, it was gone. You're a pretty lucky little guy to be living in a time like this, Sean." The small face gave no indication that the boy had heard anything that Cody had said. "Sean," Cody tried again, "are you listening to me?"

"I'm not Sean," the boy said quietly, staring straight ahead. "I'm Wolf."

"Yeah, right." Not for the first time he cursed his own impotence in dealing with his son's strange behavior. He was beginning to have doubts that he would ever get through to Sean. "You'll love the game, Sean."

There was no response.

"Wolf," Cody amended.

"Maybe," the small voice conceded, still looking straight ahead.

Desperation prompted the next words out of Cody's mouth. "Sammy Squirrel's going to be there."

Sean turned to look at his father, wary disbelief mingling with innocent joy in his eyes. Cody saw the struggle and felt it grip his heart. Ever since Deborah had died, Sean had been afraid to let himself believe or trust in anything, including his father. It ripped Cody apart to see him like this, even though he shared some of the same feelings. It was hard to believe in things when they could so quickly vanish on you.

Sean stared down at his hands, then back at his father. "Really?"

Cody thought of Lee. She certainly didn't bear any resemblance to a squirrel. "As real as he can be."

Sean fidgeted in his seat. "Can you drive faster, Dad?"

"Not without getting a ticket." Cody glanced up at his rearview mirror, searching for the familiar signs of a patrol car. There weren't any.

Cody stepped down on the gas pedal.

Chapter Three

Damn, it wasn't supposed to rain!

Lee looked over toward the group of celebrity baseball players huddled beneath one of the temporary awnings set up for the game. Not one of them was under fifty-five. A lot of them were drenched, just as she was. The sudden deluge had whisked out of nowhere, with no warning. It was abating now, but not before it had interrupted the game.

Random drops were still falling. The sky was acting like a leaky faucet that was about to give up the ghost and dry up.

It was about time.

Lee pushed her bangs out of her eyes. Soaked, they hung about half an inch longer and obstructed her vision.

She caught a glimpse of a loping, graceless scarecrow of a man who clutched a clipboard to his shallow chest. He wore a red T-shirt that matched Lee's in color and slogan—"Homeless is a terrible place to be." Calvin Reynolds was one of the program's coordinators. Calvin, Lee noted, was miraculously dry.

"You think it's okay to go on, Leanne?" Though Calvin liked to pretend that he called the shots, he deferred to anyone whose voice rang with authority, a trick Lee could easily manage.

Lee looked up at the sky. It was a sullen gray with splotches of blue. The sun was shining through the openings, creating small bundles of light that punctuated the wet field like stepping-stones. It didn't qualify as a rainbow, but Lee took what she could get.

"We'd better try to give these people their money's worth. Play ball, Calvin."

There was panic written on the long, angular face. "But I'm not—"

Sighing, she patted his bony shoulder. "It's a figure of speech, Calvin. Just go ahead." She shook her head as Calvin shuffled quickly toward the former ballplayers. It was hard to get good volunteers these days.

She looked over to the buildings behind her and the roofed archway between them. A lot of the people who had come to see the game were clustered there. The more adventuresome had dashed for the shelter of their cars. She hoped that they hadn't given up and driven away. The ticket money had long since been collected, but she felt an obligation to deliver what had been promised. Besides, the players both wanted and needed to play one last game before cheering fans who mentally saw a better game than the one actually unfolding. She hated to see any of them disappointed. Nostalgia was a powerful medicine for a whole host of ailments.

She picked up the microphone she had dropped on the table when the rain had started. "All right, folks," she announced loudly, "it looks like the rain has decided to give us a break. It's safe to get back to your seats now."

Lee watched a hesitant trickle of spectators begin to return to their seats. Californians, she had long ago decided, had a morbid reaction to rain.

"C'mon, people, you're not made of sugar. You won't melt." She lowered her voice into a breathy, appealing imitation of Marilyn Monroe. "Any melting around here will only be done to the sound of my voice."

One of the players gave her the high sign. She wasn't sure if it was a response to what she had said, or to her imitation. The man had probably known Marilyn, she thought.

There was a low murmuring as people straggled back to their seats in small groups. Lee lowered her microphone to her side and looked up at the sky again. The clouds still looked as if they could be trouble. "Keep a lid on it, okay?"

"Who are you talking to?"

Lee swung around, startled at the sound of Cody's voice. She narrowly avoided hitting the small boy next to him with the microphone dangling from her hand. Her eyes darted from the boy to Cody. A sweeping, pleased feeling washed over her before she could stop it. She had no business reacting like this to a married man.

"What are *you* doing here?" she countered.

Cody looked her over. With her hair plastered against her like a dark blond helmet, she looked younger than her twenty-six years. And with her T-shirt hugging her curves that way...

The thought that followed brought an unconscious smile to his lips.

"The studio is one of the sponsors of this game, remember? I just wanted to see how we were doing."

We. It had a nice ring to it, she thought. And so did he, on the third finger of his left hand.

"Treading water at the moment," she answered.

"Who were you talking to just now?" Cody asked again.

"God," she mumbled, looking away. No one was supposed to have heard her.

She was nothing if not unorthodox, he thought. "You give God orders often?"

Lee turned back, brazening it out. "It's a hard, thankless job, but someone's got to do it."

"She talks funny," Sean interjected, unable to help himself. He looked at the blond woman uncertainly.

Lee grinned at Cody. "He noticed."

She saw Cody's eyes skimming over her. Again strange, diametrically opposed feelings danced through Lee, confusing her.

Damn, why did he have to come now, just when she looked her worst? Just when she looked like a drowned rat that had been washed up on shore? The fact that the filled-to-capacity crowd had seen her didn't faze her half as much as the fact that he had.

The man's married, Lee. It doesn't matter what you look like. And even if he wasn't, there's no sense in asking for trouble.

There might not be any sense in it, but it was happening just the same.

Her glance shifted to Sean, who was still eyeing her curiously. "Who's your buddy?" she asked Cody.

"I'm not his buddy." The small chin lifted proudly. There was no mistaking the distance he set up between himself and his father. Lee wondered if it was just one of those things that periodically flared up between a parent and a child, or if it had more serious ramifications. "I'm Wolf."

Cody saw that Lee took Sean's declaration in stride without blinking an eye. Feeling a wave of relief and gratitude, Lee's reaction caused an instant bond to be formed between them.

Lee squatted down so that Sean didn't have to continue looking up when he spoke. "Hi, Wolf." She stuck out her hand. The boy took it hesitantly, after glancing at his father to see if it was all right. The quizzical look surprised Cody. "Are you here to see the game?"

Sean shook his head. "I don't like baseball."

Lee glanced up at Cody, amusement in her eyes. "I see you raise them honest." She turned back to Sean. "Stick with me, kid," Sammy Squirrel instructed, "and I'll show you where all the nuts are."

Cody stood back, observing the scene, amused.

Sean's mouth dropped open. "You talk like Sammy Squirrel."

Lee sniffed indignantly, still keeping in character. "I *am* Sammy Squirrel."

The small brow furrowed as Sean tried to understand. "Sammy's shorter and he's got a tail."

Lee rose and put an arm around Sean's shoulders. She looked around to see if anyone was listening. "Wolf," she said, her voice low, "do you know about Batman?"

Sean cocked his head. "*Everybody* knows about Batman." He paused. "What *about* Batman?"

There was an edge of suspicion in his voice that was foreign to the voices of most five year olds. What had happened to him? Lee wondered, her emotions stirred in sympathy. "He has a secret identity, right?"

"Right," Sean answered warily.

"Well, I'm Sammy Squirrel's secret identity."

Childish enthusiasm warred with fear of disappointment. "Really?"

Lee crossed her heart solemnly. "I never lie to a short person on Saturdays." She took his hand conspiratorially.

To Cody's surprise, Sean didn't pull his hand away. Lee was making more strides in three minutes than he had made in the nine months since Wolf had appeared. The woman's a witch, he thought. Wolf and the Witch. Nice title for a short story. Cody's smile spread.

"So, where's Mrs. Lancaster?" Lee's question was a bit too breezy-sounding for her own ear. She saw the muscles in Cody's jaw tighten. Well, that certainly had been the wrong thing to ask.

Cody looked away and fixed his attention on something far off. "My wife died thirteen months ago."

Open mouth, insert foot. Nice work, Lee. "Oh, I am so sorry, Mr. Lancaster." She glanced at Sean's face and began to understand the reasons for his behavior.

Cody turned to look at her. She did look genuinely sorry. Why? She had never known Deborah, never knew the sweetness, the kindness that had been Deborah Wainwright Lancaster.

When she made a mistake, she did it royally. Time to retreat. "I, um, have a habit of talking a little too fast and a little too much. If you'll excuse me—" She started to edge away.

"No, wait." Cody didn't want her running off just yet. She had cracked the shell around Sean and that in itself was worth any price to him. Besides, she had no way of knowing about Deborah. It had been merely a harmless query on her part.

Cody cleared his throat. "You didn't answer my earlier question. How's it going?" He gestured around the field.

"We've had a pretty good crowd today, as you can see." She purposely avoided his eyes, still smarting from her error. "And, until the rains came down, we were doing pretty well."

She looked at the bleachers that formed a semicircle around the field. They were nearly full again. She let out a sigh of relief. "For a minute there, though, I thought we'd have a stampede on our hands." She turned her face toward him without thinking. A quick grin curved her mouth. "I guess Californians never get used to rain."

Cody laughed. "In New York, it's the expected, not the unusual."

They were talking about the weather. Not exactly earth-shaking. But at least it was better than nothing. He seemed to have forgiven her for her invasion of privacy. "I've been meaning to ask you about that."

She was leapfrogging from topic to topic, he thought. "About what?"

"You've just moved here from New York, right?"

"Yes." That was a matter of record. Now what was she driving at? Cody noticed that Sean seemed to be hanging on her every word, where usually he drifted off into his own mental fog. She was doing something right. Several somethings, Cody amended.

"For someone straight from New York, you don't sound, well, you know," she shrugged, helplessly looking for a way out, "New York-y."

Her observation amused him. *She* amused him. He folded his arms before his chest. "I don't, huh?"

She shook her head. Another wet strand slapped her face. Resolutely, she pushed it back.

"No. If anything, you twang." It wasn't exactly the most eloquent way of describing the soft, Southern lilt in his voice, but it got the idea across. Words were failing her today. She watched Cody lift a brow that she found herself wanting to trace with a fingertip.

Get a grip, Lee.

"Quite a student of accents, are you?"

She caught his amusement and, far from being offended, went with it. "Voices are my life," she said with a sexy French accent.

"You happen to be right." He looked again at Sean, but the boy was rooted to the spot, studying Lee closely. "I was in New York for six years, but I'm originally from Texas. Dallas."

The image of a cowboy riding his horse fast and hard flashed through her mind. Questions rose in her mind, questions that had to be put on hold because there were other things demanding her time at the moment. Like the celebrity game.

And they should be put on hold permanently, Lee. You don't want to get involved here. It's safer playing Russian roulette with all the chambers filled.

She searched for something innocuous to say. "Nice place, Dallas."

"You've been there?" She had piqued his interest.

"Only through the magic of television every Friday night." Lee saw Calvin signaling madly from the other side of the stand. She raised her hand and waved back, as calm as he was frazzled. Calvin frowned and waved harder. "Excuse me," she said to Cody and Sean, "I think I'm being frantically waved at."

"I could see how that might happen," Cody murmured under his breath.

But Lee heard him. "Usually, it's highway patrolmen waving me over to the side of the road. This is a new experience." She looked down at Sean and ran her hand over his blond hair. "I'll be back in two slaps of a beaver's tail, Wolf," Sammy Squirrel promised the boy.

"Is she really Sammy's secret identity, Dad?" A trace of doubt lingered in Sean's voice, but Cody detected almost a plea to be convinced.

Cody watched the way the pockets on Lee's jeans moved up and down as she walked away from them. His fast-talking deejay certainly had an incredible figure. "The lady is everything she says she is."

Sean scratched his head, still apparently confused as to what to believe.

Cody laughed and hugged the boy to him, then raised him into his arms. For the first time in what seemed like years, he began to see the light at the end of the tunnel, and it wasn't the headlight of an oncoming train. Things *were* going to work out, just as his sister had predicted. With no small thanks to a very unusual lady who spoke in magical tongues.

"Come on, Sean, let's go watch Lee in action."

Sean rested his hands on his father's collar. "But her name is Sammy."

"Shh, we're not supposed to let people know that, remember?" Cody warned, savoring this intimate moment.

Sean nodded his head solemnly. The secret was safe with him.

Standing next to Calvin, ironing out a last-minute problem, Lee watched Cody and Sean move into the stands. It made a nice picture, father and son.

After satisfactorily answering Calvin's myriad of questions, Lee went back to offering random comments on the game and the plays. This half of the game was hers. Another voice characterizer from the studio had been the commentator for the first half.

He's available.

The sentence drummed itself over and over in her temples, totally independent of the words she was uttering for the benefit of the crowd.

He might be, but she wasn't, she reminded herself. Not to him, not to anyone. She couldn't afford to be. He might as well have been married. It would have been a lot better for her if he was.

The rain stayed at bay throughout the rest of the afternoon. The only indication that it had rained was the drops that still lingered on some of the greenery surrounding the perimeter of Crawford Hall, catching the sun within the borders of its orbs, creating tiny rainbows.

By the end of the game, Lee was thoroughly exhausted and close to hoarse. She had completely thrown herself into the game, cheering first one side, then the other. Lunch had been a candy bar bought after a long wait in line at one of the three vending machines housed near the gym. She had lost track of Cody and Sean after the seventh inning and surmised that they had had enough of the game and had gone home.

Just as well, Lee told herself as she gathered together her notes on the vital statistics of the celebrity players. *The less you see him, the better you'll both be for it.*

"Hey, Lee."

She turned to see Foxworth McCord, known as the Silver Fox in his playing days, walking her way. In his left hand he held a baseball.

Lee stopped packing and leaned her hip against the table that had been set up for her. "You played a great game, Foxy."

Foxworth waved a well-tanned, wrinkled hand. "We *remember* a great game." He winked. "But it was fun, I'll grant you that." Beneath the fine lines that were etched in around his eyes and mouth, he beamed and suddenly looked young again. "The guys and I all wanted to tell you how much we appreciated you getting us together for this game. We haven't had so much fun in years. It's nice to do it for a good cause."

He squinted and looked down at the baseball in his hand, a wave of nostalgia passing through his eyes. "Sure beats the pants out of doing dog-food commercials."

"I *like* dog-food commercials," Lee said with a grin. "Some of my best friends are dogs."

The old player shook his head. "You, lady, could make friends with the devil himself. I know, 'cause I've seen you talking to Whitney Baxter." He nodded toward a bent, departing figure on the playing field wearing a striped blue-and-white uniform and a blue cap pulled low over a partially bald dome.

"Whitney's a dear," Lee teased, holding back a grin. She knew exactly what Foxworth meant. As a young player, Whitney had had one stunning season he never let anyone forget.

"Huh!" Foxworth snorted. "That so? Can't wait for hunting season to start. Hey, here I am, running off at the mouth when all I wanted to do was to give you this." He thrust the baseball toward her. "This is for you. We all signed it."

Lee took the baseball from the hand of the man whose arm was once heralded as being golden. Her eyes misted slightly. "I don't know what to say."

"But you will, Lee. Sure as the sun's gonna shine, you will." He chuckled then leaned over and brushed dry lips against her cheek. "Take good care of yourself, kid." He began to walk away. "If you ever need some dog food for one of your 'best friends' just give me a holler. I've got cases of the stuff." He waved to her as he disappeared into the crowd.

She had never seen him play in his prime, but she knew that he had to have been something special. He still was.

"You feed your best friends dog food?"

Lee jumped and swung around, looking straight into Cody's eyes. It was an unguarded moment, and something strong and sexual telegraphed itself to her. Something warm and sensuous and utterly dangerous for her self-preservation. She wanted to enjoy it. But she knew she shouldn't. Ambiguous feelings began to jockey for position within her. This wasn't good. "Why don't you wear squeaky shoes?"

"They wouldn't squeak on the grass. Besides, I wouldn't get to hear half the interesting things that I do if I wore them." With Sean before him, Cody rested his hands on his son's shoulders as he spoke. "For instance, I wouldn't have learned that you put this thing together. I thought this was the foundation's idea."

Lee pretended to look for someone in the dispersing crowd. She wondered if Cody had seen anything in her eyes in that one moment. There was a hunger within her, a hunger that would always have to go unsatisfied. She had given in to it once and reaped a harvest of bitterness. She wasn't about to be foolish again, no matter what the need. "It was their idea. But someone had to come up with it for them."

She really was a whirling dervish, he thought. "I see." Lee was so totally different from his wife. And yet he could see similarities, even at this early stage.

Lee looked up at his face. Did he see? she wondered. No, she doubted it. He saw what he wanted to see. No one saw the whole picture. She wouldn't allow that.

"It goes along with your Crusader Rabbit image," Cody added.

Sean dragged his attention away from Lee to look up at his father. "Who?"

"A cartoon character way before your time," Lee explained. She felt more at ease talking to Sean than to his father.

"Yours, too," Cody pointed out.

"No cartoon is before my time." Lee laughed softly. "It's a neglected art form."

Three students who looked as if they majored in weight lifting picked up the table behind Lee and carried it past her and Cody. Lee was forced to move closer to Cody in order to get out of their way. Cody didn't step back soon enough and their bodies touched marginally. More wasn't needed. Their eyes held in wonder as both felt something that could only be classified as a jolt spring between them. Lee broke eye contact first, suddenly interested in the state of the grass beneath her feet.

"What's she talking about, Dad?"

"I'm sure we'll find out in time," Cody replied. "Need a ride home, Crusader, or is Rags coming for you?"

The grin that rose to her lips came naturally. "You *did* watch cartoons."

"Would a general production manager for a major cartoon studio admit otherwise?"

Lee was tempted to say something flip in return, but wasn't sure if she should. Sometimes she used discretion, although not often.

"So," Cody continued, "if Rags isn't coming, my offer to take you home still stands."

She hesitated. It wasn't wise, and she knew it, knew *herself*. There was a need within her that struggled to the fore every so often, prompted by seeing family gatherings such as this. The fact that Cody was better-looking than a man had a legal right to be and could stir any woman's dreams just added to the problem.

"Can we take you home?" Sean chimed in. "Please, Sammy? It's okay to call you Sammy when nobody's around, isn't it?"

But then, why should she start being wise now, at her age? Besides, it was only a ride home, and there was a child between them. What could happen? Nothing, absolutely nothing.

"Yes, you can call me Sammy even if there is someone around. And as a matter of fact, I do need a ride home." She placed one hand on Sean's shoulder. "My car wouldn't start this morning. I had to come in with Alex Anderson, and I'd really rather not have to repeat the offense if at all possible."

Cody looked around. He saw Alex in deep conversation with a very nubile spectator who seemed to be hanging on his every word, as, it appeared, was Alex.

"That bad?" Cody asked.

"Not if you don't mind genuflecting before you get into the car." Alex worked in the production end of the studio and had a very high opinion of his sexual prowess.

"Let's go. You've put me in the mood to rescue a fair damsel in distress." Cody took her arm as he escorted her from the field.

Lee decided that there would be nothing wrong in enjoying this for just an afternoon. A person couldn't get hooked on something in a single afternoon, right?

She had a nagging, nebulous feeling that she should have realized that she had just passed her first danger sign. And failed to heed it.

Chapter Four

As they approached Cody's Jaguar, Sean pulled open the door on the passenger's side and began to climb into the front seat.

Cody placed his hand on the boy's shoulder, stopping him. "Why don't you let Lee sit there, Sean? You can ride in the back."

Sean looked at him sullenly.

The last thing in the world she wanted to do was create an awkward situation. "I've got a better idea, Mr. Lancaster." She saw Sean turn toward her and watch her carefully. A bright boy, she thought. A boy not to be patronized. Sammy Squirrel rode to the rescue. "Why don't Wolf and I sit in the back together? I bet he's got some neat forest stories to tell me."

The change in Sean's expression was something that should have been captured on film, Cody thought. The dark, pouting look vanished instantly, almost as if it had only been a figment of Cody's imagination. A smile, an actual smile, took its place in response to Sammy's suggestion. Cody had begun to give up hope of that ever happening. He regarded Lee for a long moment. Maybe he should take this woman home with him.

Cody walked around the hood to the driver's side and opened the door. "It's all right with me, except for one thing."

Lee was already hustling Sean into the back and climbing in herself. She stopped, one foot inside the car, her hand on the door, and looked at him quizzically. He had conditions for people who wanted to ride in the back seat? "What's that?"

"It's Cody," he told her with a warm smile that she seemed to bring out of him with no effort whatsoever. "Just Cody."

There was no "just" about this man, not by a long shot. "To everyone?" She hoped he didn't notice the suspicion in her voice. Then again, maybe it would be better if he did—just in case he had plans.

What was she driving at? Cody wondered. Was there a reason she didn't want to be singled out? The lady was giving out some very mixed signals that he was having difficulty reconciling.

"To everyone over the age of ten." Without further discussion, Cody slid in behind the steering wheel.

Lee sat down next to Sean and closed the door. Because he had neglected to, she pulled out Sean's seat belt and buckled him in.

"I guess that qualifies me," Sammy decided, taking care of her own seat belt next. "I'm eleven." She saw Sean gaping at her in wonder. "Just be sure you don't drive Wolf and me to the nearest zoo," she warned Cody.

Cody caught Lee's eye in the rearview mirror as she turned to talk to Sean. Cody grinned. The lady was definitely intriguing him.

A small shaft of guilt penetrated his consciousness as Cody realized that he *was* interested in the woman riding in the back seat of his car and talking up a storm with his son.

Who would have believed it?

Not him, that was for sure. Cody had truly believed that he had found everything he had ever been looking for in Deborah. After she had died, it had been very difficult for him just to put one foot in front of the other. When he had finally pulled himself together, he had assumed that he would go on working, taking care of Sean and living a productive, quiet life. Women, relationships, those were things that he honestly believed were beyond him, something in his past. He had had his love, had been blessed once and would move on with memories that would sustain him for the rest of his life.

That he found himself interested, responding, actually *thinking* about a woman as anything other than just another human being, was an unsettling revelation. It told him that he couldn't make safe assumptions about anything, not even himself.

Nothing was written in stone.

He glanced again in his rearview mirror as he turned the car onto the city's main drag. "So, where is it that I'm chauffeuring you to?"

Lee stopped talking and looked at Sean thoughtfully. "Think Yosemite's too far away?"

Sean raised and lowered his thin shoulders. He hadn't the vaguest idea where Yosemite was, but knew that it was a park of some sort. If this laughing lady wanted to go there, it was okay by him.

"Yeah, it's too far," Sammy declared. "I guess I'll settle for home." She leaned forward and, in her own voice, gave Cody her address.

Her breath warmed his neck and stirred him again. His hand tightened slightly on the wheel. "Is that an apartment complex?"

"No, a residential area. A patio home, to be exact."

Cody turned slightly in her direction as he braked for the light. "Really?"

She wondered why he looked so surprised at that. "Yes, why?"

A patio house sounded too mundane for someone like Lee. She made him think of a gypsy, moving restlessly from place to place. Maybe it was the fact that she never seemed to stand still when he talked to her. Even now, as she spoke to Sean, she was gesturing with her hands and constantly shifting in her seat. A house was too stationary for someone like that.

He shrugged. "No reason. I just thought that forest creatures might tend toward furnished apartments, that's all."

She laughed, forgetting for a moment to be on guard. "This was a deal I couldn't resist. Even squirrels have their price."

Lee didn't add that the real reason was because she had always wanted to have a home of her own. Nor did she say that roots, something she had never really had, were her heart's main desire. So, she had bought a house and made it into a home, her own home, arguing with herself that she didn't need the comfort of a marriage to make it real. Certainly her parents hadn't. They were two wonderful people until they came in contact with one another. They had failed miserably at the institution, as had her sister, Donna.

As had she.

When Cody glanced at her again, he saw a strange expression on her face, as if she was miles away. And sad about it. He wondered if something he had said had made her react like that.

"So," he asked, "what's wrong with your car?"

Lee cleared the fog from her brain to answer his question. "It won't go."

Cody laughed. "That's like saying *Moby Dick* was a book about a whale."

She saw nothing wrong with that. "Well, it was," she pointed out. Sean grinned at her, as if showing her that he was on her side, though he couldn't know what she meant.

Cody shook his head. She obviously didn't get the idea. "The description is missing substance."

"And my car is missing a mechanic. I have no idea about cars, Mr. Lan—" She saw one brow raise in the mirror. "Cody," Lee amended.

Why should saying his first name make a difference to her? she wondered. Why did it sound so—personal, so seductive on her tongue? There wasn't a reason in the world why it should. Maybe keeping all her characters straight in her head was making her muddled. She certainly was having trouble thinking clearly this last week.

"All I know," she continued, "is that I put gas into it, stick a key in the right place, and it takes me where I want to go."

"You're right." Cody nodded. "You don't know anything about cars."

She shrugged, looking out the window. They were almost there. "I know all I need to know."

Cody made a decision. "Maybe I'll check it out for you when we reach your house."

Lee looked up sharply. The idea of having him over to her house made her panicky. "No, please."

She sounded almost distressed. No, he had to be hearing wrong. Must be all those birds out there, screeching to one another. "Why, is it shy?"

He did have a sense of humor, she thought. Why did that please and panic her at the same time? What *was* wrong with her? Cody Lancaster was just a nice man, that was all. Why couldn't she relax?

Because she thought she liked him.

She liked the President too. Having him offer to come over and fix her car wouldn't have put her into such a tailspin, she told herself.

Calm down, Lee chastised.

"No." She did her best to keep her response nonchalant. "But you must have something more important to do."

Sean tugged at her T-shirt. "No, we don't," he told her when she looked at him.

Lee knew when she was cornered. "Out of the mouths of wolves." She threw up her hands in surrender. "Okay, if you really want to get dirty, who am I to stop you?" The quick grin she saw sent a funny shiver through her stomach. Maybe she was coming down with the flu. She fervently hoped so. Lee looked at the boy at her side. "Do you help him fix cars, Wolf?"

The fact that she used his name of choice went a long way toward winning Sean permanently over to her side. He didn't even seem to notice that she was no longer speaking with Sammy's voice.

"No." He shook his head so hard, his long, straight hair bounced.

Lee leaned toward Sean and said in a pseudo whisper, her eyes on the rearview mirror, "Well, I don't think you should stand still for letting him hog all the fun." She thought for a moment. What *could* Sean safely help with? "Maybe he'll let you pop the hood."

Sean immediately slid forward and grabbed on to Cody's headrest. "Can I, Dad?" There was eager enthusiasm in his voice.

Cody's eyes made contact with Lee's in the mirror. How did she do it? he wondered. And could she teach him? "I don't see why not."

A sign proclaiming her street came up, but Cody made no move to get into the right lane. "Wait," Lee cried, "you almost missed it!"

Cody made a sharp turn that sent another ripple through her stomach and would have gladdened a policeman's heart and ticket book had one seen them. "Not for the world, Lee. Not for anything in the world."

She stared at the back of his head. He wasn't referring to the street he had almost passed by. She could tell. Just what *was* it he wouldn't have missed?

And why did that simple statement make her uneasy?

"You live here?" Cody couldn't keep the surprise out of his voice as he brought the car up the small, tidy driveway. The single-story gray-and-blue house looked more or less like all the others in the tract, fresh, but not exceptional.

"You were expecting maybe a fun house?" Lee climbed out of the car and held the door open for Sean. The boy darted out and stood next to her.

Cody let the car door slam behind him as he passed his hand over his face. "I wasn't sure what to expect." At least, he hadn't been expecting anything so normal-looking. The house even had a front yard with a patch of white daisies bordering it on both sides of the entrance.

Lee grinned, one corner of her mouth rising a little higher than the other. "Then you'll love the trapdoor in the family room."

Cody looked at her. "What?"

"Only kidding." But the way she winked gave Cody pause. He'd have to check it out later.

He nodded toward the garage door. "Your car in the garage?"

"Unless it decided to run away from home, yes." Lee took out her key and opened the lock. Lee raised the door on the two-car garage. Her car stood in the middle of a garage that brought new meaning to the word *clutter*.

"Wow," was Sean's assessment. It sounded like a positive one to Cody. How could one person collect so much junk?

Cody glanced at her sideways. "I take it you're part pack rat."

Gary Cooper warned in reply, "Smile when you say that, partner."

"Who's that? Who's that?" Sean wanted to know, thinking it was another cartoon voice.

It was apparent that the boy was already beginning to know his way around Lee. That made Sean one up on his father, Cody thought.

"Gary Cooper," Cody answered. He raised his eyebrows in a silent question to Lee. Had he guessed correctly?

Lee was impressed. "Very good. Do you like old movies?" It was the only reasonable assumption to make. She adored them.

"Yes," he answered without thinking. "Deborah and I—"

Abruptly, Cody's voice trailed off. He didn't want to talk about Deborah at a time like this. He didn't want to spoil it for Sean. But one look at the boy told him that Sean hadn't even heard him. Cody let out a sigh of relief. "Sorry," he murmured to Lee, dragging a hand through his hair.

Lee felt a twinge of envy. Theirs had probably been the only marriage that had ever worked out. Lee turned away before he could see the wistful look she knew was in her eyes.

"Why don't I pull out the car for you?" Sean followed her like a shadow. She waved him back. "Stand aside, boy," ordered Sheldon Snake, a pompous character from Sammy's world, "or I'll flatten you like a pancake and have you for breakfast." She raised and lowered her eyebrows. "Yessss."

Sean giggled as he jumped aside. "She's fun, Dad," he whispered to Cody.

"She certainly seems to be," Cody agreed. "Also absent-minded." He watched her get into the car and then just sit there. "What's the matter?" he asked needlessly.

She craned her neck around to see him. "I forgot. It won't start."

Cody nodded. "I was wondering when you'd remember that. Well, it's a cinch I can't work on the car while it's in there." He scratched his head, thinking. "Put the car in neutral."

She glanced around the interior of the car. "In what?"

"Neutral. Release the parking brake and move the gear shift to the letter *N*," he prompted.

Cody was having trouble finding a way to move around to the front of the car. There were boxes and bags obstructing him any way he turned. With effort, there was just enough space for him to work his way forward. "I'm going to push the car out. You steer."

"Okay."

Cody gave a hard shove. The car began to coast backward. "The brake," he cried, following her out. Any moment, the car was going to pick up speed and wind up in the house across the street. "Hit the brake, Lee."

Jamming her foot down and yanking at the emergency brake, Lee got the car to stop just before it rolled into the street.

"Good reflexes," he muttered as he came around the side of the car.

"I try."

Lee got out and handed him the keys. Cody pocketed them without thinking. "How did you manage to pack that car in there?" Cody marveled, nodding toward the garage. Looking back, there hardly seemed enough space for a car, and even now things were toppling so as to fill the opening left behind.

Lee grinned. "Magic."

Sean's eyes widened into huge circles. "You do magic, too?"

Lee touched the boy's ear and then moved her fingers in a circle before him, handing Sean a coin. The look on her face was innocent. "Doesn't everyone?"

"Not like you," Cody observed.

Lee felt herself getting warm as his compliment registered. But then Sean was tugging on the hem of her T-shirt again, claiming her attention. She blessed him for it.

He clutched the coin possessively in one hand. "Can you make a rabbit appear?"

"Let's see you get out of this one," Cody murmured out of the side of his mouth, only loud enough for her to hear. He was just as curious as his son was to see what she'd do next.

Lee shook her head solemnly. "Sorry. I can't do that around you."

Sean's brow furrowed. "Why?"

"It just wouldn't be fair to the rabbit." Her voice was the soul of logic. "Everyone knows that rabbits are afraid of wolves."

Sean nodded sagely. He hadn't thought that there'd be a drawback to being a wolf. "Oh, yeah, right." Lee ruffled the boy's hair, and he grinned up at her.

Cody was impressed. She was quick, both physically and mentally, it seemed. He couldn't help wondering if she was quick in everything she did. He decided that it would be best for all concerned if he turned his attention back to the car.

"Very nice recovery," he commented as he passed her.

She was obviously proud of herself. "I thought so."

Lee watched as he circled her car slowly, studying it. She knew it wasn't very much to look at. "Will you need anything?"

"No, not yet." Cody sat down inside the car and turned on the headlights. "Besides, I don't think you could readily find anything even if I did in that, um—"

"Mess?" she supplied, amused. She knew her limits and made no apology for them.

"You said it, I didn't. See any lights?"

She glanced down. The headlights were very faint. "Just a glimmer." He wasn't about to get away that easy. "But you were thinking it. It's not so bad," she lied. "I found the car, didn't I?"

He laughed, shaking his head as he got out again. "That was luck."

Lee put her hands on her hips and pretended indignation. "Not by a long shot. I've had twenty-six years of practice finding things other people lost." Crouching, she placed two fingers on Sean's lips, one at each corner and gently pushed up, forcing his mouth to curve. "Like smiles." She was rewarded by Sean with a grin of his own volition.

"I see what you mean," Cody murmured. Gratitude was evident in his words. "C'mon, Sean, you said you wanted to pop the hood." He held the car door open for his son. Sean scrambled around the rear, eagerly looking inside the car.

"I think it's the handle right next to the steering wheel on the left," Lee prompted, watching father and son pool their resources. "See, I know something about cars." She grinned as the hood popped open.

"I don't think that knowing how to pop the hood qualifies you as an expert." Cody laughed and then began to look around the exposed area.

Lee peered over his shoulder. All she saw was a dirty collection of hoses, wires and metal. She wondered how Cody could make any sense of it. "Sure you don't need anything?"

Cody turned, unaware that she had been standing so close. It caught him off guard for a minute. There was a long look between them that said a great deal which neither one of them could put into words, or knew how to at the moment.

"No." Cody turned away, slightly shaken and more than a little confused by his reaction. "I have tools in my trunk."

"Do this as a sideline when general managing is slow?" Lee asked.

He laughed. "I like fixing cars. It's a hobby. My first car was a 1968 Mustang my Dad gave me in high school. I spent more time under it than I did *in* it."

She tried to visualize Cody as a teenager, sweating over a car he probably loved passionately. It made her smile. "I guess that gives us something in common."

He looked up. "How's that?"

It was very obvious to her. "You like fixing cars, and I have one."

She certainly did like simple answers, he thought as he pushed up the sleeves of his jersey. He wondered if that was really true. Did she like simple answers? Was she as cheerful, as uncomplicated, as she presented herself? He thought there was something he had detected in her eyes, something that made him believe there was a lot more to the lady than was evident at first glance. A riddle, he mused.

It gave Cody something to look forward to.

Gingerly, he examined the battery terminals. They looked corroded. "How old is your battery?" He couldn't find an installation date on it.

Lee stopped to think. "Six months. Maybe a year. Maybe more."

Vague. Could he have expected anything else? "You're sure of that?" he asked dryly.

She hadn't heard him. "What?"

"Never mind." He waved away his comment. "Do you have any baking soda?"

Baking soda? "Are you planning to make brownies?"

Sean giggled at her question. His father never baked anything. They had a housekeeper who did that sort of thing.

"No, I'm going to see if I can get your car to run. Baking soda?" he repeated. Cody began to think that perhaps he was asking for the impossible.

"Maybe." She remembered using some in the laundry a month or two ago when she had run out of softener. It was probably still on the utility shelf. "Let me look." She took two steps toward the interior of the garage, then looked over her shoulder at Sean. "If I'm not back in two days, be sure to send a search party in for me."

"Can I help?" Sean asked eagerly.

Lee glanced at Cody. "Brave son you have here."

"Yeah, I'm pretty proud of him." Cody grinned, but his answer was serious.

Sean gave his father a curious look before following Lee. Cody went back to disconnecting the battery. The terminals were absolutely caked with grit and dirt. "Oh, and get me an old toothbrush if you have it."

Lee stopped and turned around, staring at Cody. "Batteries have teeth?"

"Just bring it."

She shrugged and looked at Sean. "He always this demanding?"

Sean shook his head as he followed her through the narrow space left by the car. "Naw, he's pretty easy, most of the time."

"Like him a lot, don't you?" She could hear that in his voice.

Sean stopped and thought over his answer for a minute. Since his mother had died, his father had stopped being any fun. He looked off into space a lot and didn't play with him anymore. It had made Sean twice as sad and lonely before he discovered how to get lost in his own little world. "He's okay, for a dad."

Reaching the shelf, she began to rummage through the assortment of boxes and cans. "It's not easy being a dad."

"How would you know?" It didn't strike Sean as something that a girl would know about. Even if she *was* Sammy Squirrel's secret identity.

Lee turned around and put one hand to her chest, her fingers spread apart and resting lightly against her. She lifted her chin slightly. "I know many things of this world and others."

Sean's eyes nearly popped out of his head. "Wow, that's Princess Enchantra! She's real cool."

Lee took it as her due, or at least Enchantra's. "Thank you," she said regally.

"Are—are you—?" Sean's words became tangled.

Still in character, Lee bestowed a smile upon the awestruck subject. "I am."

"Hey, Dad!" Sean yelled.

Cody started, narrowly avoiding hitting his head on the inside of the hood. "What?"

"She's the Princess, too."

Cody had absolutely no idea what princess Sean was referring to. "Of course she is," Cody called back, wiping his hands on the back of his jeans. "She's that and probably a hell of a lot of other things, too."

And he had a feeling he was going to find out about all of them in time.

Chapter Five

Presenting Cody with the baking soda and the toothbrush he had requested, Lee left him to do whatever it was that a man did with a toothbrush and baking soda while hovering over a car battery.

Sean began trailing after her as Lee turned to go into the house. "Why don't you keep an eye on your dad?" she suggested gently. "He might need some help."

Sean was momentarily crestfallen. His father was there every day. Sammy Squirrel wasn't. But the idea of being able to help his father work on the car *was* tempting. Maybe they could do things together like they used to do. "Okay." Sean darted back to Cody, his face eager.

Cody glanced toward Lee and smiled his thanks. Satisfied that she had done her best to promote good father-son relations, Lee went into the house.

Circumventing Pussycat, who was stretched out in the middle of the floor, she made her way to the refrigerator. "Some watchdog you are," she muttered under her breath. "You're supposed to bark when you hear strangers, remember?" She shook her head fondly at the sleeping animal.

She searched through her refrigerator, moving aside cans of soda, vegetables and odd-shaped items wrapped in aluminum foil. Her bare arm was beginning to feel very cold by the time she pulled out two large cylinders of prekneaded cookie dough that unconditionally promised heaven with chips in ten minutes.

"Provided, of course, one can successfully mount these things on a cookie sheet," she mused, reading the label. She cracked open one container and laid out the long tube of dough on the counter.

Pussycat raised his head, sniffed the air and moved closer to her side.

"Wondered when you'd get up." She pulled out three cookie sheets and placed them on the counter. "Smell of cookie dough get to you, Pussycat?" As an afterthought, she took down the faded red apron that hung on the side of the refrigerator and hastily tied it around her waist. Pussycat watched every move intently. "Sorry, you're going to have to share this with my guests."

Ignoring Pussycat's expression of intense anticipation, Lee concentrated on cutting the dough into tiny pieces. She had just finished arranging them all on the sheet when Sean burst into the room.

"We've fixed your car!"

Lee had barely enough time to place the cookie sheets into the oven before Sean grabbed her hand and pulled her out the front door and over to his father.

Her car engine was idling. "It's fixed?" Lee looked at Cody in mild disbelief.

Cody looked down at his hands. They were filthy. "Yes, it's fixed. The cables weren't making good contact with the terminals."

"And all it took was a toothbrush and baking soda?" she asked incredulously.

So much for trying to get technical. "Don't forget the most important ingredient—expert knowledge."

She liked his sense of humor and the way he pitched in to help. She liked him, dammit. She liked the fact that he seemed to care about his son. She liked, and therein lay the problem. Lee struggled to keep a firm grip on the exuberance she felt bubbling up within her.

Remember, you tend to overreact to kindness, Lee.

Remembering didn't provide sufficient braking power to overcome her speeding. "I wouldn't dream of forgetting something like that. Expert knowledge is a rare commodity. I'll keep your phone number handy for the next time my garbage disposal explodes."

Cody wasn't about to ask her to explain that. He was no fool. He looked at her apron. "Have you suddenly decided to go domestic?"

She grinned and tugged on the apron hem. "No, this is just a vestige of temporary insanity. I have no idea how to go about cooking and cleaning like normal mortals."

Sean sandwiched himself in between them to get her attention. "Why don't you just use magic?" He looked up at her innocently.

Cody couldn't help grinning at Sean's question. "Yes, why don't you?"

Lee tried to ignore Cody's sexy grin. She tried to ignore the feelings it awoke within her, feelings and dreams. Dreams about things she had once wanted so passionately and believed possible. There was no use in thinking about things that would have to stay out of her reach.

"Magic should never be used for personal gain," Enchantra informed Sean, with an eye on Cody. He appeared to be as entertained by her ensemble of different voices as Sean was.

Sean shook his head the way he had seen his father do when confronted with something that was awe-inspiring. "Boy, she's good." He drew out the last word.

Lee wanted to hug Sean and eat him up where he stood, but restrained herself from showing the full extent of her reaction. Attachments, she knew, could be fatal.

Cody nodded. "My feelings exactly," he pronounced, "Se—Wolf."

Sean flashed his father a surprised grin at the correction.

Cody's eyes met Lee's over the small, flaxen head. He saw the look of approval. The woman was a total enigma. One moment, she was like a small, impetuous child, behaving like the Road Runner on megavitamins, the next she was some sort of a sage psychologist, expertly guiding a reconciliation between him and his son.

Just who and what *was* Leanne Sheridan? He realized that he definitely wanted to know more about her than could be found in the pages of the personnel file at Hayward Studios. Cody had a feeling that he wasn't going to get that kind of information out of her. Not voluntarily. There seemed to be an edgy nervousness about her each time he drew closer to her than she allowed.

"To get back to your question," Lee said, "no, I haven't gone domestic. I just thought that since you and Wolf came to my rescue twice today, I should at least feed you cookies."

Cody laughed. "Really know how to wine and dine a guy, don't you?"

Lee glanced at his hands. Despite the dirt, or perhaps even because of it, they looked like manly, capable hands. Hands that would be quick to hold and comfort and— Lee roused her mind and handed him the kitchen towel that she had slung over one shoulder.

"Wining and dining is done in restaurants. Besides, homemade cookies are far more personal, don't you think?" Cody wiped his hands and gave her back the towel before reaching in the car to turn off the engine. She took it and turned on her heel. "This way, gentlemen." She held the front door open for them. "Try not to let Pussycat trip you."

"Pussycat?" Cody asked. It didn't sound like a very creative name for a cat, given Lee's nature.

"My dog."

"Of course." That was more like it.

Cody looked around slowly as he entered. It was a very cozy house. Cozy and warm and a total extension of the woman now leading them to the kitchen. The furniture in the living room was large, overstuffed and looked exceedingly comfortable. The three pieces, in a semicircle around an overly wide coffee table, left very little room for foot traffic.

A deep, rumbling bark met them as they walked into the kitchen.

"Pussycat?" Cody guessed as the dog stood up on his hind legs and began to lick Cody's face.

"Pussycat," she confirmed.

"He's beautiful," Sean exclaimed excitedly, petting the dog so hard Lee could almost hear the strokes.

"Shh, don't let him hear you say that. He thinks he's vicious-looking. Down, Pussycat, you're mauling my boss," she warned.

Obediently, the dog dropped down on all fours and padded back to his post by the oven. He watched as she removed the cookies.

The kitchen table, moved against one wall, was barely large enough to accommodate three people. Sean pulled up a chair and planted himself in the middle. As he moved the chair in, he banged against a table leg. A pile of open letters, still in their envelopes and leaning against the wall, fell over, spilling all over the table.

Cody picked them up mechanically. Every one of them appeared to be from some sort of charitable organization, asking Lee for a contribution. Fascinated, Cody flipped through them quickly. There was everything in the pile, from institutions providing beds for the homeless, to schools that educated native Americans, to clubs asking for donations to help save endangered species.

Lee, Cody thought, stacking the letters together, was an endangered species. He didn't think that he had ever met anyone like her. He would have definitely remembered if he had.

He looked in her direction as she was carefully removing the hot cookies. "Certainly get more than your share, don't you?"

Lee stifled a yelp of pain as her fingertip came in contact with the hot sheet. She wanted to stick the offended finger in her mouth, but didn't. Wincing was her only luxury. "What's that?"

Cody held several of the envelopes up in the air. "Junk mail."

She shoved the cookie sheet farther back on the counter and pulled out a spatula. "That's not junk mail. Junk mail is when someone tries to give you a toaster oven in order to entice you to come watch a travelogue on investing in swampland in the Ukraine." She muttered an oath under her breath as one cookie crumbled rather than be separated from the cookie sheet.

Cody wondered if the dog would be bald by the time they left. Sean was steadily rubbing the same spot as he continued petting the incredibly docile animal. "They don't have swampland in the Ukraine." Not that that fact would mean anything to her, he thought.

Lee looked at him over her shoulder and frowned. She waved an impatient hand in the air. "Oh, you know what I mean."

"Oddly enough, I do." Maybe her condition was catching, Cody mused. He was actually beginning to understand her a little.

"This—" she nodded toward the restacked pile on the table "—is where they offer you the chance to feel good about yourself."

And then again, maybe he wasn't. Cody sighed. "Would you like to explain that a little further?"

Lee brushed aside her bangs with the back of her hand and turned from the counter, holding a platter full of cookies. Not exactly heaven with chips, she thought, but close. She placed them on the table in front of Sean.

"Sure." She looked at Cody. "There's no better feeling than the one you get when you know you've helped someone." She broke off a piece of a cookie and tossed it to Pussycat, who moved just enough to catch it, then settled back at Sean's feet.

"I see." Cody picked up one cookie that was a shade darker than the others and studied its unusual shape. "How do you choose—between charities I mean?"

Lee picked up a small, ugly-looking cookie and bit into it, hoping no one had seen it. "I don't." Rather than sit, she rested a hip against the table and nibbled on the cookie. Cody had the impression that she probably ate most of her meals that way. She took another bite. "I give a little to everyone."

"What's left over for you?"

Lee blinked. It was so obvious, she didn't know why he was asking. "Happiness."

The lady was getting more complicated by the minute, Cody mused. A wisecracking woman with a heart of gold. Quite a combination. But then, he reminded himself, her file had alluded to that. He just hadn't actually believed it, that's all.

Cody decided to press a little. "You can't live on that."

She shrugged, giving him a wide grin. "I can. On that and cookies."

Her answer was flippant, but in an odd way, it satisfied his curiosity about her intentions. Apparently, she was for real. And all the more enigmatic for it.

Cody leaned toward her as his son devoured his third chocolate chip cookie. "How about happiness of a more personal nature?"

She felt something tighten inside her abdomen. A warning. "Giving is personal."

So, they were going to waltz around this, too. She was quick-witted. He didn't stand a chance. He wouldn't get any information she didn't want to divulge, Cody decided. "Is there anyone special in your life?" He couldn't believe that he had actually been that blunt. He had overstepped his bounds. Cody almost felt embarrassed.

Yet he needed to know.

Slowly, Lee dusted off one hand against the other. Pussycat ignored her, satisfied with getting his crumbs from Sean. "Sure."

"Oh." Cody thought it was absolutely ridiculous that he should feel disappointed. But he was.

"Wolf," she couldn't help adding. Lee ran her hand over the boy's hair. Tearing himself away from Pussycat and the cookies, Sean grinned at her, his lips outlined in cookie crumbs. Lee picked up a napkin and brushed them off.

"Oh." His disappointment faded instantly. Cody didn't bother questioning it.

Lee looked at him sharply, catching the intonation in his voice. In another lifetime, she thought, maybe, when dreams did come true, when things didn't dissolve into mist, she would have been tempted to see if there was something here beyond a very intense chemistry that kept nudging at her. But she didn't have another lifetime. She only had this one, and she had learned from her failures and disappointments.

"You're not eating," she pointed out. "Wolf is going to get them all."

Cody looked at the platter. Sean hadn't even put a dent in the pile. "I doubt that. There's enough here for an army."

She straightened and looked over toward the pantry. "I'll get you a doggie bag." Lee glanced down at Pussycat, who had raised his head again. "No offense, Pussycat."

It completely amazed Cody the way she addressed dogs and people in the same manner, as if they were on the same level. Except, he noted, that she didn't seem nervous around the dog or his son. But she was nervous around him.

He watched her move hurriedly to the pantry. "Are you trying to get rid of us?"

Lee took out a paper sack, brought it over to the table and held it open with one hand as she slid the cookies off the platter with the other. One casualty landed on the floor, to be salvaged and devoured by Pussycat.

She was being too eager. "No. Um, would you like a tour of the house?" Lee folded the top of the sack down and placed it on the table next to Sean. "There's not much to see, but I thought that maybe Wolf would like to see my family room."

She caught Sean's attention instantly. "With the trapdoor?"

Lee glanced at Cody. "He doesn't forget anything, does he? Actually," she told Sean, "there *is* something there that you might want to see." Lee led the way out. Cody and Sean followed, with Pussycat coming in their wake.

Why was she suddenly so nervous? Cody wondered. Because he had asked a few personal questions? She didn't strike him as the type to be leery of personal questions. She seemed too open, too up-front for that. And yet, there it was, a veneer of restlessness that he could only classify as nerves. Did *he* make her nervous? It seemed like a ludicrous idea, and yet what else could it be?

"And this," Lee announced in Robin Leach's voice, as if she was leading a grand tour through an estate, "is the world-famous family room. The trapdoor, however, is at the cleaners.''

Sean stopped petting Pussycat long enough to shoot a quizzical look at his father. ''You can do that with trapdoors?''

''Apparently,'' Cody answered.

But Sean was no longer listening. He was making a beeline for the huge stuffed animal that was standing in the corner of the room like a giant trophy. Sammy Squirrel, in all his splendor, stood grinning back at Sean. Sean threw his arms around it and dragged it back to Lee, nearly falling over with his burden. Pussycat carefully lingered behind the boy, eyeing his rival.

Cody moved to catch Sean, but the boy managed to recover his footing. ''Sean, that doesn't belong to you. I don't think—''

''It's all right.'' Lee shook her head to stop Cody from taking the toy back. She saw a look of pure ecstasy on Sean's face. That was enough for her. ''They seem to be meant for each other.''

Cody looked at her in amazement. ''You're not giving it to him.''

She blinked. ''I'm not?''

''You are?'' Sean squealed with joy.

Lee squatted down to Sean's level. ''I think you can give him a better home than I can.'' It had been a gift to her from the studio, celebrating her third year with the cartoon ensemble. But the look of love in Sean's eyes made parting with it almost essential. ''You seem to be just the right height.''

''Can I, Dad?'' Sean's question was muffled against the rust-colored fur.

Lee rose to her feet. ''He's housebroken,'' she told Cody, ''and doesn't eat much.''

Outnumbered and thoroughly entertained, Cody held up his hands to ward off any further persuasion. "Far be it from me to break up such a good match." He searched Lee's face to see if she was only being polite. He assumed that the stuffed animal meant something to her. Why else would she have kept it? "As long as you don't mind." But he saw no trace of hesitation or dismay in her eyes. Instead, they sparkled with pleasure.

She watched as Sean first hugged the stuffed animal and then turned to confer with Pussycat about his acquisition. "I'd mind if you said no."

Cody regarded her thoughtfully. "Yes, I think you would."

Aware that he was staring at her, Lee shoved her hands into her back pockets. "I suppose the rest of the house would be anticlimactic, now."

Oh no, you're not getting rid of me that easily. "Not if you want to show it to me." Cody looked over his shoulder at Sean, who was on the floor, surrounded by his two new friends. "I think we can leave Sean out of this for now. He seems to be occupied."

Lee licked her lower lip. "Okay."

The small action left a sheen on her lips. They looked moist and soft. And exceedingly tempting. Cody tried to think of something else. It didn't work. He wanted to kiss her.

Maybe if he talked about Sean, he thought, following her down the hall. There *was* something he had to know. "How do you manage to do that?"

She paused, her hand on the doorknob of the next room. "Do what?"

Cody nodded back at the family room. "Get Sean to come out of his shell."

She shrugged. It wasn't something she consciously thought about. "It just comes natural, I guess. Most kids think of me as just another big kid, anyway. I'm one of them."

"No," Cody said quietly, "I think you're one of a kind."

Lee turned to look at him. His blue eyes were dark and mysterious in contrast to the genial expression on his face. He scared her. What he was stirring inside of her scared her. "Don't flatter me, Cody."

It almost sounded like a plea. Cody didn't understand. What was it that she was afraid of? It couldn't be him. That would have been ridiculous. No one was afraid of him. "Why shouldn't I flatter you?"

The troubled expression on her face vanished as she tried valiantly to regain her composure. "Because I might get to believe it."

He wanted to reach out and touch her. To feel her skin beneath his fingertips. She was so mercurial, so unusual, he had a need to prove to himself that she was real. But he had a feeling that to do so would send her bolting away. A moment ago, she had seemed brassy, strong. Yet now he felt that she needed to be protected. She stirred an entire kaleidoscope of diametrically opposed feelings within him. He'd never felt this way before. He needed to understand what was happening here.

"Why would that be so bad?"

She shrugged, wishing that he would drop the subject. She couldn't tell him any more than she already had. "It just would."

"Lee." Lightly, he touched her shoulder and felt the tension. He let his hand fall. "I get the feeling that I make you nervous."

She moved down the hall. "You're my boss. All bosses make employees nervous." And besides, she thought, you could still fire me and ruin *everything*.

"Uh-uh." It wasn't anywhere nearly that simple, and they both knew it.

"Uh-uh?" she echoed, lifting her chin pugnaciously, looking for a cartoon character's voice to toss in his path. None materialized. She had to make do with Leanne Sheridan, who was sinking fast. "You've done a paper on the subject?"

"No, but I don't think my being a boss has anything to do with it. I think my being a man does."

"And another shy, retiring man heard from." She was being as flip and light as she could, desperately trying to break the mood that was taking hold of her. Of both of them.

Lee groped for the doorknob behind her. She pushed open the door, not bothering to look into the room. She wanted to get this over with as fast as possible and send him on his way before anything happened.

"This is my bedroom." She shut the door before she finished the sentence. "I sleep here."

Okay, he'd play along. "And this?" He pointed to the room next to it.

She opened the door. "My guest room. I guest here." She turned around. "Look, Cody, maybe—"

But it was too late for maybe. She had turned so abruptly that she brushed right up against him. Cody took hold of her waist instinctively, his fingers curving around it and pulling her toward him. He was on automatic pilot and flying into the side of a mountain.

He *was* making her nervous. It only heightened the mystery around her, making him more determined to find answers. Her very personality seemed to energize him. Knowing her for this last week, being around her, had almost single-handedly brought him out of the deep doldrums he had been wandering in. It was as if she had burst into his dark world, carrying sunbeams in her hand and scattering them aimlessly.

But he didn't want it to be aimless. He wanted her magic or whatever it was to be directed toward him. He wanted to explore all this, especially the feelings she generated in him. Most of all, he wanted to know why he frightened her.

And why, in a way, she frightened him. Maybe, he realized, it was because, in being intrigued with her, drawn to her, he was closing the book on a chapter of his life.

But he didn't want to reason it out right now. He just wanted to kiss her. Cody slowly slid his hands up her sides until he framed her face.

Lee held her breath. More accurate, it had stopped, dead, in her lungs. The "it" she was afraid of happening was going to happen. He was going to kiss her and she knew that she wanted him to. Very much. Fear licked at her, fear that he wouldn't. And, oh Lord, fear that he would. Right now she could only speculate about her reactions to him. If he kissed her, she'd know for sure.

And be sunk for sure.

No more mistakes, she thought desperately. Please, no more mistakes. The only way to avoid that was not to let him kiss her.

Too late.

His lips had found hers, floating down to them so gently that it totally destroyed all hope of her making a break for it. You couldn't make a break for it with melted limbs.

She forced herself to go dormant inside. Icy. She wasn't going to let this be anything more than another part of his skin touching hers, like a hand or a foot or a—

No foot had ever felt like this. Against her will, her arms went up around his neck as her body swayed against him. Reason had fallen headfirst into a paper shredder.

Cody had been curious. And perhaps a little needy. What he hadn't been was prepared. But how did one prepare to be sucked straight into a whirlpool? One didn't. One let it happen and hoped to God that he could survive.

Lee fought valiantly to regain her wits. But she was losing the battle and losing it faster than the speed of light.

Oh no, it couldn't happen again, she thought. *Not again.*

It was happening.

And yet this had never happened before, not like this, not so quickly. Not where she couldn't breathe, think, or function at all. Not where she wanted to sell her soul to keep the kiss from ending. She wanted to cry, to run, to survive. She could only stay where she was, drowning and loving this one instant in time for which she would pay so dearly.

He had slammed into that mountain he had been flying toward. Thoroughly shaken, Cody held her against him as he broke away. There was a small child in the other room to remember. For a moment, that was all he could remember. He waited until the pounding had left his ears.

Lee clung to him. She knew she shouldn't, but she had to. If she didn't, she was going to fall. It took a few seconds for the blood to return to the rest of her body. It had been totally drained a moment ago. "I think the warranty on my lips just expired."

Cody drew back and looked at her. He reminded himself that while she claimed to have a large repertoire of voices, she had never claimed to be sane. "What?"

She hoped she could keep her voice steady. "You know, when warranties expire, things fall apart, they disintegrate. Are my lips on fire?"

"No." He laughed.

She drew a deep breath, then let it out again. "Funny, the rest of me is." She grinned, hoping that he wouldn't notice how much effort it took, and tapped him on the chest. "You should come with a warning label from the Surgeon General."

Cody released her. "Aren't you ever serious?"

"I *am* serious." She turned and cocked her head, listening. "Is that Sean?"

Cody listened for a moment. There was nothing. "I don't hear anything."

"I do." And it was a cry for help. But it was coming from inside of her. "I'll go see what he wants."

Cody watched as she hurried away, then followed her silently.

Chapter Six

When he reached the den, Cody found Sean, one arm wrapped around the stuffed animal, the other on the dog, looking up at Lee with eyes that threatened to pop out of his head.

"I can really come and watch?" Sean's enthusiasm was reminiscent of the boy he had been a year ago. Cody felt another flash of gratitude. Lee was working miracles, accomplishing in an afternoon what he hadn't been able to do in thirteen months.

With Sean in the room, Lee was able to to relax again. Cody had thoroughly shaken her foundations. Her carefully constructed walls had fissures throughout and, for a moment there in the hallway, had threatened to collapse. She needed time to regain her footing.

Lee placed her hand on the boy's shoulder. "If your father says it's all right."

"If his father says *what* is all right?" Cody asked, though he knew, seeing the look on Sean's face, that he would have been hard-pressed to cite what he *wouldn't* agree to. It was worth absolutely everything to see Sean looking so alive and happy again.

Lee turned at the sound of his voice. She looked totally composed and at ease. Cody wondered if he had somehow imagined the entire incident in the hallway. Lee exhibited none of the wariness he had seen barely seconds ago. The idea of her being afraid of him, for whatever reason, now seemed totally laughable. Maybe he was suffering from delayed jet lag.

Perhaps he *had* imagined the wariness, but he hadn't imagined the passion. That had been there, and it had knocked the breath out of him. And the impression wasn't about to fade away.

Lee saw Cody looking at her curiously. It took a lot for her to continue maintaining her facade. He had caught her off guard before, played upon her weaknesses, weaknesses he probably had no idea that she had. With strict vigilance on her part and any luck, nothing like that would ever happen again. She'd just have to be more careful, that was all.

She opened her mouth to explain what Sean was talking about, but the boy was faster.

"Lee says she can take me to the studio so I can see how they make the cartoons talk." The words tumbled out over one another. Sean hugged the stuffed squirrel so hard that both nearly fell over on the dog.

Cody reached out and steadied his son. It hadn't occurred to him that Sean would be interested in coming down to the studio with him. He had thought of it in strictly practical terms, as work. Seeing it from Sean's angle, there might be some magic for a little boy to glean around there after all.

"I told Wolf that he could come along and watch me work if he'd like." Her long dark lashes swept up, and she gave him a sweet, innocent look, knowing very well that Cody couldn't say no to this. "As long as you approved."

She liked the idea of taking Sean with her. She'd always been fond of children and Sean needed someone besides his father right now. She wanted to help, to make a difference. "I can go AWOL from the studio for a little while and pick him up after school if you give me the address and permission."

Cody saw Sean watching him, his young face intense, waiting for the answer. "Sure, I have no objections to that."

"All right!" Sean clapped, and Sammy, unsupported, pitched forward.

Lee grabbed the stuffed animal before it had a chance to fall on Pussycat. "Yes," Lee said, grinning at the boy, "I think it is."

"Would you mind if I tagged along, too?" Cody asked. He had already monitored her work. But the situation had changed somewhat. He wasn't asking her as the general production manager, he was asking as himself. There was a difference. A big one. He could have sworn that something small and guarded flittered through her eyes. Again.

"Sure." Her voice sounded tinny to her ear. Lee lowered it an octave. "The more the merrier." There was absolutely no reason why she should feel nervous about this. He had already observed her, hadn't he? He was just coming along with his son, that was all. Nothing more than that.

And yet, she knew that she was lying. She tried to tell herself it was because she was still worried about her job, but it was more than that. Much more.

Cody looked at his watch. He'd promised Thelma that they'd be home early. Though she was his housekeeper, she thought of herself as part mother and moved about the house, muttering under her breath how they made her worry if they returned home late.

He tapped the stuffed squirrel lightly on the head and looked at Sean. "Why don't I carry your friend to the car, and then you and he can wait for me? I'd like to talk to Lee for a minute." Hefting it, Cody tucked the squirrel under one arm and led the way out of the house.

Sean dawdled behind, dragging one foot in front of the other, wanting to stay where he was. Lee nudged him forward. When he looked at her, she winked, then pointed toward the door.

"You mean Sammy," Sean corrected his father as he caught up to him.

Cody glanced over his shoulder at Lee. She was failing miserably at covering up an amused grin. "Whoever she is."

Lee held open the front door for them as Cody, Sean and Sammy trooped past her. She collared Pussycat and made him stay with her. "See you Monday, Wolf," she called out after the boy.

Sean turned and waved to her before following his father to the car.

Lee crossed her arms before her chest, hugging herself as she stood and watched the two of them go. It was going to be all right for them.

But she could feel the uneasiness returning. If she held a tight grip on herself, she lectured silently, it was

going to be all right for her as well. She should have
never let things get to where they were. She knew better. He had just taken her by surprise. She was prepared now. Everything would be just fine. She was in
control again. She knew the penalty for believing that
relationships could work out. Tears and grief. Relationships *didn't* work out, not in the long run. Sometimes not even in the short run. She had prayed long
and hard that her parents would stay together. For a
time, they did, and there had been nothing but chaos
while they had. But at least they had parted civilly at the
end.

That hadn't been her lot.

Involuntarily, she shivered, remembering. The scars
she bore from her own marriage had stayed with her a
lot longer than the stinging imprint of Lloyd's hand on
her cheek. If she kept reminding herself of that, the way
she had felt as he had constantly berated and belittled
her, she wasn't going to go off rowing over the falls in
a skiff made of paper and dreams.

Cody settled Sean and the large stuffed animal into
the back seat, solemnly strapping a seat belt around
each, much to Sean's delight. "You stay put, okay?"

Sean looked at his traveling companion. "I will if
Sammy will."

"Sammy," Cody warned the grinning squirrel,
"don't move a muscle."

Sean stifled a giggle.

She was right, Cody thought, closing the car door. It
was going to be all right.

Cody tried to assess what was going on in Lee's mind
as he turned back to her. But it was hopeless to even try.
He hadn't the vaguest idea what went on in there.

His eyes on her face, he dared her to step away. He had guessed right. Lee held her ground. "Thank you for Sammy." He nodded toward the occupants in the back seat of his car.

Lee rested her hand on Pussycat's head, subconsciously seeking some additional strength. "My pleasure."

"And for Sean."

"Wolf," she corrected. The soft smile on her lips made Cody yearn to take her in his arms again.

"Wolf." He had to remember to call Sean that until the boy decided to become his son again. He hoped it wouldn't be much longer.

"Don't thank me for him, he's not mine to give," Lee pointed out, her voice soft, melodic.

So this is what she sounded like when she wasn't hiding behind all those cartoon voices, he thought. He liked the sound of her voice. It had an almost innocent quality to it. He felt something protective stir within him. He wondered if she'd laugh at that. Or be drawn to it. Did she need protecting? He didn't know, but he sensed she needed someone to love her. As did he.

Aware that he was studying her, Lee turned away to look at Pussycat. She scratched the dog affectionately. Pussycat didn't ask anything of her. He was just there to love, and love back without the accompanying recriminations she had come to expect.

"He's always been yours, Cody."

Cody shook his head. It had been a hard road to travel the last few months. "Not if you'd seen him this past year." He leaned his shoulder against the doorjamb. "He was very attached to his mother."

He was standing too close. She was reacting. She was prepared, and she was still reacting to him. This was

going to be more difficult than she had imagined.
"Most small boys are. He's probably afraid that the
same thing is going to happen to you now."

The thought took him by surprise. "Me?"

"Yes." She looked at him, momentarily forgetting
that he had the ability to entangle her in an awful lot of
trouble. Sean was important. Cody had to understand
what was going on in his mind. "He's afraid of losing
you. In his child's mind, he probably thinks that if he
pretends he doesn't care, that it doesn't matter what
happens to you, that when you leave him, it won't
hurt."

She took a step toward the car, peering into the back.
Sean saw her and waved again. She waved back, then
turned to look at Cody. "Let him work this thing
through and just be there for him."

He watched the way the crisp autumn breeze played
with the ends of her hair, swirling wisps about her face.
"Will you be?" He knew it was a lot to ask, but he
needed someone to help.

Lee grinned. Her heart had already been lost to the
small boy. "At his beck and call."

She meant it. He was glad, but he couldn't help
wondering why. She'd only met Sean today. "What
makes you such an expert on children?"

"Not an expert." For a moment, she looked off in the
distance. Old feelings returned, dragging sadness in
their wake. "I just know how it feels to lose a parent, a
home."

He had been clumsy and he hadn't meant to be. He
didn't want to stir up any painful memories for her.
"Oh, I'm sorry."

She realized by his tone that he had misunderstood.
"Oh no, no one died." Without thinking, she placed a

hand on his arm, as if to physically relieve him of his embarrassment. "They got divorced, which, in a way, I guess, made it a little worse." An enigmatic smile played on the corners of her lips. "Two homes for the price of one and neither one complete." And she didn't feel wanted in either. It had been several years since she had seen her parents.

Lee stopped abruptly and dropped her hand. She didn't usually talk about her past, or her parents' divorce. He couldn't really be interested. Why in heaven's name was she telling him all this?

She shifted and moved back to the shelter of her doorway. "Well, I'll see you Monday."

She was backing away, he thought. He hadn't been wrong before. There was definitely something more to her than the glib voices, the bright, breezy style. Leanne Sheridan came in layers. Cody found himself wanting to undo them, to strip her down until there was no more pretense between them.

"Monday," he repeated.

As he walked to the car, whistling, Cody realized that he was finally getting on with his life. And liking it a great deal.

Sean gripped Lee's hand tightly as she ushered him through the cavernous soundstage. She had told him that she was taking him to the engineering booth where they laid down tracks for the cartoons. He thought that was funny because everyone knew that trains, not cartoons, ran on tracks, but he liked her too much to tell her she had made a mistake.

Parts of the stage were kind of dark and spooky-looking, swallowed up in shadows. But he wasn't really frightened, Sean thought, tightening his hold on her hand. Not really. He knew Lee would protect him. After all, she was part princess. He'd seen what Enchantra could do when the evil warlord challenged her.

There was so much to look at, Sean didn't know where to look first. "Is this where you live?"

"No, you were at my house on Saturday, Wolf, remember? This is where they draw all the cartoons. They're not ready for the next take yet, so if you'd like, I can show you the place where they draw Sammy." She saw a look of disappointment come over his face. Concerned, Lee stopped walking. "What is it, Wolf?"

"You're not really Sammy, are you?"

The sad tone made her want to cry. Dreams died hard, even little dreams. She crouched down to Sean's level. "I am a little. I'm his voice."

But that didn't change the facts. "But he's not real, is he?"

Oh no, she wasn't about to be the one who made him question the existence of Santa Claus and the tooth fairy. Not yet. Dreams were things that were destined to fade all too soon. Five was too young to face too many harsh realities, and he had already suffered more of a loss than he should have.

Lee put her arm around him and pulled him closer to her. "Oh, Sammy's real all right. As long as you believe, here, in your heart—" Lee traced the tip of her finger over Sean's red shirt, outlining a heart "—he's very real and will go on forever. I know I believe in him." *I just don't believe in happy endings, that's all,* she added silently.

The smile that rose to Sean's lips satisfied her. In his own childish way, he understood. Lee rose to her feet. "Ready?"

Sean nodded eagerly and quietly followed her to the art department.

For the next half hour, she led Sean from desk to desk where he solemnly observed the techniques used to give his favorite cartoon character depth and color.

The personality, one older cartoonist told Sean with a wink, was up to Lee. Sean looked up at her almost reverently.

When it was time for her to get to work, Lee sat Sean up on a stool in the back of the sound booth. Crossing his heart, he solemnly promised to be as silent as a wolf stalking his dinner. Then he watched, fascinated, as she and a tall, willowy man she had introduced to him as Henry became Sammy and Shadoe right before his eyes. There were other people in the booth who did things with huge machines that looked like they had a thousand buttons on them, but Sean only had eyes for Lee and her partner.

Though Sean now thought he understood that she wasn't really Sammy, as far as he was concerned Lee was still making magic.

"You were very good," Lee told Sean as she helped him off the stool at the end of the session. Though it had only lasted sixty-five minutes, she was surprised that he had managed to be quiet for so long.

"Thanks." He beamed at the praise.

Setting Sean on the ground, she looked down at him. "So, Wolf, how did you like seeing the way cartoons are made?"

Confidently, Sean took her hand as they walked off the soundstage. He was going to be a heartbreaker for sure, she thought, given another twelve years. She wondered what he'd look like then. Probably a lot like his father.

"It was neat." Sean looked up at her, his eyes shining. "I really liked the way you got the bad guy." She had figured he'd like that part. Then Sean appeared to be thinking something over. He was quiet for a minute before he blurted out, "Um, Lee?"

Pushing the heavy outer door open, Lee blinked a little as they stepped out into the brightly lit hallway. "Yes, Wolf?"

Sean bit his lip and worried it a little before making up his mind. "You can call me Sean if you like."

She put her arms around him and hugged, hard. "I like." Why was there such a lump in her throat? She'd known it was just a phase for him. "I like very much. Can your dad call you Sean, too? I think he kind of likes the name better, anyway."

"Yeah, I guess so."

She released him and dusted off the knees of her jeans when Sean suddenly looked past her shoulder and cried, "Hey, Dad, you missed it. She was great!"

Lee swung around to see Cody standing behind her.

"I take it I'm too late to see Sammy do his thing." He felt a twinge of disappointment. The meeting with one of the studio's accountants had run longer than he had anticipated. Cody had hurried to soundstage seventeen as soon as the meeting was over, but he was obviously too late. He had been looking forward to being able to enjoy the taping for a change, seeing it through Sean's eyes instead of the eyes of a general production manager whose main concern was the monetary end of the operation.

Lee was surprised to see that Cody actually did look disappointed. Maybe there was a little of the small boy in him, too. The thought made Lee smile, though she wasn't aware of it. She didn't think that Cody could possibly be interested in the taping because of her. Lloyd hadn't been, even though he had said he was. Lloyd had said a lot of things that had made her fall in love with him. A lot of things that hadn't been true. She didn't take things at face value any more. She was older and wiser now.

Or, at least older.

"I would have thought you would have had enough of watching us work," she told Cody.

"Not from a purely entertainment point of view." Casually, he placed one hand on Sean's shoulder and one on hers. "Can I take you home?"

"I have my car," she pointed out. "Which, I might add, you fixed beautifully. It purrs like a kitten."

For Sean's benefit, she imitated a car purring like a kitten. Sean clapped his hands together and laughed. His autographed original inked cel of Sammy and Shadoe that one of the cartoonists had presented him with floated to the ground. Lee was quick to pick it up and return it to Sean.

"No harm done," Lee said in response to the worried pucker that furrowed his small brow. She tousled his hair with a laugh.

Cody didn't want her to leave. Not so soon. He hadn't felt like this—this exhilarated, this alive—since he was a teenager. Since he had first seen Deborah. Though as far as personalities went, the two women were as different as night and day, Lee had still given him a reason to look forward to each morning again, a different reason than just going on because Sean depended on him.

She made him happy to be alive.

"I'm glad to hear the car's running so well." *Think of something, Lancaster, before she pulls another vanishing act.*

"Well, I guess I'll see you—" Lee began to edge away, but he caught hold of her arm.

"Since I missed your performance," he continued quickly, "I have another idea. Why don't we follow you home, you leave your car there, and we'll go out for dinner?"

"What does missing my performance have to do with dinner?" she asked, puzzled.

He was floundering and he knew it. "Nothing," Cody admitted honestly, "but I'm new at this. Don't crush my ego, okay?" She opened her mouth to say something, but Cody was getting faster. With her he found he had to be. "It's my way of paying you back for all those cookies."

Lee shook her head. "I was paying you back for fixing the car, remember?"

He shrugged good-naturedly. "We can keep this up indefinitely. Who knows where it'll lead?"

She knew. She knew exactly where it would lead. And she didn't want to go there. Once was enough.

Though she wanted to go out with him, she knew she couldn't. Lee began to make an excuse, but then Sean chimed in, "Please, Lee?"

Helplessly, she looked from one Lancaster to the other. "You're both asking me out?"

Cody ruffled Sean's hair. It felt good to be able to do that again. "Looks that way." This wasn't exactly what he had in mind. He had wanted to spend some time alone with her, but if this was the only way he could get her to agree, so be it.

HOW TO VALIDATE YOUR
EDITOR'S FREE GIFT "THANK YOU"

1. Peel off gift seal from front cover. Place it in space provided at right. This automatically entitles you to receive four free books and a lovely pewter-finish Victorian picture frame.

2. Send back this card and you'll get brand-new Silhouette Romance™ novels. These books have a cover price of $2.69 each, but they are yours to keep absolutely free.

3. There's no catch. You're under no obligation to buy anything. We charge nothing–ZERO–for your first shipment. And you don't have to make any minimum number of purchases–not even one!

4. The fact is thousands of readers enjoy receiving books by mail from the Silhouette Reader Service™ months before they're available in stores. They like the convenience of home delivery and they love our discount prices!

5. We hope that after receiving your free books you'll want to remain a subscriber. But the choice is yours–to continue or cancel, anytime at all! So why not take us up on our invitation, with no risk of any kind. You'll be glad you did!

6. Don't forget to detach your FREE BOOKMARK. And remember...just for validating your Editor's Free Gift Offer we'll send you FIVE MORE gifts, *ABSOLUTELY FREE!*

YOURS FREE!
*This lovely Victorian pewter-finish miniature is perfect for displaying a treasured photograph– and it's yours **absolutely free**–when you accept our no-risk offer!*

▶ Four BRAND-NEW romance novels
▶ A pewter-finish Victorian picture frame

PLACE
FREE GIFT
SEAL
HERE

YES! I have placed my Editor's "thank you" seal in the space provided above. Please send me 4 free books and a Victorian picture frame. I understand I am under no obligation to purchase any books, as explained on the back and on the opposite page.

(C-SIL-R-04/93) 315 CIS AH7R

NAME

ADDRESS   APT.

CITY   PROVINCE   POSTAL CODE

Thank you!

DETACH AND MAIL CARD TODAY!

"Well..." Lee grinned at Sean. "A lady can never have too many gentleman admirers."

"Is that yes?" Sean looked from Lee to his father, confused.

"That's yes," Cody told him.

He sounded as if he thought he had won the battle. "To dinner," Lee felt compelled to interject. She glanced at her wristwatch. "Why don't you give me a half an hour's head start?"

Sean tugged on his father's sleeve. "I don't know if we should, Dad. That's what Sammy said when he was trying to trick the hunter into letting him escape."

Cody looked at Lee. There was a hint of amusement in her eyes. There was also something else. An apprehensiveness he was coming to expect. "Lee's not Sammy," Cody explained quietly, watching her eyes as he spoke to Sean, "and I'm not a hunter, Wolf."

A lot you know, she thought, keeping the smile fixed on her face.

"It's okay to call me Sean," Sean told his father.

"What?" For a minute, the chess game between Lee and himself was forgotten. Cody looked sharply at Lee. "How did you manage this?"

She shrugged, her hands spread wide in denial. "I had nothing to do with it. It was Sean's idea."

Brought to you by the miracle of Lee-of-the-many-voices, Cody thought. The look of thanks he flashed her said it all.

She wasn't used to gratitude, not from a man, at least not from a man she felt something for despite all her best efforts to the contrary. She wasn't certain how to react.

Lee looked away. "Half an hour," she repeated. Then, cupping Sean's face in one hand, she lifted his chin slightly and promised, ''And I'm not leaving town.''

''We'll hold you to that,'' Cody called after her.

Damn you, she thought, hurrying to the parking lot and her car.

''C'mon, Sean, we'll stop by my office for a minute and then get ready to take Sammy out.'' He draped his arm around the boy's shoulders.

Sean hugged his autographed picture to his small chest and grinned up at his father.

This was stupid, Lee told herself as she dashed through her front door and raced toward the bedroom. She was getting sweaty palms over nothing. Absolutely nothing. Cody Lancaster was just an attractive man. The world was full of them. So what?

She stopped and looked into the mirror over her bedroom bureau, as if to catch herself in the lie. A *very* attractive man, she amended, who was merely taking her out to thank her for being nice to his son. There was nothing more in it than that.

She yanked out a skirt and a pale blue pullover sweater from the closet, then slipped off her shoes. Hurriedly, she wiggled out of her jeans, kicking them aside next to the shoes.

What about the kiss?

That had been nice, she was forced to admit. Very nice. Okay, more than nice. It had been wonderful. But she wasn't about to get carried away, she promised herself, shoving her arms through the sleeves of her blue pullover. Men kissed women all the time; that didn't mean anything at all. That was just hormones.

Why was she making such a federal case out of it?

And why, she asked herself as she looked down at them, were her hands shaking?

Poor circulation, that was all. And then she laughed as the full implication of her line came to her. Maybe *that* was the problem. After her divorce, she hadn't circulated at all, hadn't dated, not even casually. There had been nothing for her but work, work and more work, to erase the horrible memories.

So why, with that as her background, she asked herself, slipping the straight white skirt on, was she walking headlong into the lion's den again? Why was she crawling onto the platter and offering herself up as an hors d'oeuvre?

She didn't have an answer. There was no time for one. They were here. The doorbell was ringing.

"Probably a death knell," she muttered to Pussycat, buckling her belt as she went to answer the door.

Chapter Seven

"This isn't exactly what I had in mind." Cody raised his voice to be heard above the din. He leaned his shoulder against the corner of the arcade game that commanded Lee's attention. Her expression was intent and wondrously rapturous as she shot down alien after alien that flashed across the screen. Sean was watching her every move as if he was memorizing them.

When he had suggested that they go out together to a restaurant, Cody hadn't envisioned one whose decor incorporated long wooden tables and benches, scores of active children and games designed to keep them clustered and out of the dining area for chunks of time bought by quarters that were thrust into metal slots.

Lee spared Cody an amused glance before she went back to making the universe safe from invading aliens. "Don't you like pizza?"

Actually, he did like pizza. Shared in the quiet of his den, with an old movie flickering across the large screen in the background. Not served by a waitress stuffed into a rodent costume and wearing drooping whiskers affixed to her face.

"Yes, but—" He got no further in his explanation as he saw Lee tense.

She jerked the video stick to the left and knocked out an entire squadron which exploded into a multicolored meteor shower. Swiftly, she shifted the stick to the right to avoid colliding with the meteors. "Then it's the video games you don't care for?" she guessed.

Cody didn't mind video games. They were divertingly interesting and fun in their place, although he wasn't very good at them. What he minded was the fact that Sean had shanghaied Lee the moment he had eaten his fill of pizza, begging her to show him how to play Alien Showers. That had been half an hour ago.

"Lee, it's not the game, it's—" The next danger had Lee waving Cody to hold his thought for a moment. With a patient sigh, he gave up.

Distracted by Cody, Lee found herself caught in the next shower, and her last life dissolved in a swirl of bright lights. Her grand total score blinked on the screen.

"Sean." She turned, surrendering the joystick to the boy. "It's your turn now."

Hesitantly, Sean curved his fingers around the stick and looked at the screen. "Wow, look at that score!" He turned to Lee. "You get to put your name into the game. Forever. You're famous!"

As he said it, her first name, which she had typed in at the start of the game, now appeared in the third-place position, behind someone named Chris H. and Tony P.

Lee grinned as she blew on her fingers like an old-fashioned Western gunfighter who had just outdrawn his opponent. "When you're good, you're good." She winked at the boy, stepping to the side. "But it takes lots of practice." Lee dug into the front pocket of her jeans and handed Sean several quarters. "See what you can do with these."

Sean slipped in the first quarter, then looked at Lee hopefully. "Can you watch?"

Lee raised her eyes to Cody, waiting for his answer.

"We'll watch from here." Cody pointed behind Sean to the table where their pepperoni pizza, only half-consumed, was waiting for them.

Taking Lee by the elbow, Cody gently but firmly guided her to the table. "He's still answering to Sean," he marveled.

Lee sat down and turned so that she could see Sean clearly. She waved, and the boy returned to playing the game. "I think perhaps Wolf's gone back to his lair permanently."

"I still don't know how you managed that." The other day, when Sean had asked her, Lee had claimed to be able to perform feats of magic. Cody was inclined now to believe her. She certainly had worked magic with Sean as far as he was concerned.

Lee shrugged. "There's nothing to it, really. Just patience."

Cody shook his head. He had been patient. Infinitely patient. It hadn't been enough to reach Sean. It had taken whatever that special something was that Lee had to offer to lure Sean out of his withdrawn state.

He smiled to himself. Just as it had taken that same "something" to pull him out of his. He had existed, worked, worried. But he had only been moving through the shadows of life until Lee had suddenly appeared, talking in all those funny voices of hers, creating images that made him laugh. And made him want.

"It took a hell of a lot more than that, and I think you know it." Cody looked over toward Sean. The boy's small brow was furrowed as he tried to concentrate on wiping out an array of blinking, colored lights that were supposed to be the enemy from some distant cosmos.

Cody jerked a thumb at him for Lee's benefit. "He didn't look that alive even a week ago."

His attention returned to Lee. There was something about her that just seemed to radiate and touch people. When they had come in, it had taken very little for her to be drawn into a one-on-one contest with Sean. And though she seemed to be trying her best to win the skeetball toss, Sean was the winner each time by just enough for it to be believable. They had attracted the attention of an entire assortment of children, and Cody had lost her for a while. But he didn't mind. He rather liked watching her, a petite Pied Piper in the middle of an appreciative pint-size audience.

But now he wanted her to himself. He wanted to find out what made her tick. And retreat. Looking at her sitting next to him, he couldn't find a trace of the woman he had kissed yesterday, the woman who had backed away, apprehensive of something he couldn't see. But Cody knew that she was there.

"I was hoping to go somewhere where I didn't have to shout to be heard."

"You're not shouting now," she pointed out.

"No, I'm not." He leaned in closer, a smile on his lips. "But I'm going to have to stay this close to you in order to continue to accomplish that."

"A man's gotta do what a man's gotta do." She laughed softly, stifling a shiver that zipped down her spine because Cody's warm breath had touched her ear.

Cody shook his head and laughed. "You're the voice behind a dozen cartoons, a magician, a radio personality, the avid collector of antiques—"

She grinned, knowing he was referring to the state of her garage. "You mean the collector of junk."

He liked the fact that she didn't take herself seriously when she easily could. "Whatever. That's quite an eclectic combination for one person."

"Always keep them guessing, that's my motto."

Her hand rested casually on the table. Slowly, he moved his fingers along it. He felt her pulse jump. "I'd say you've succeeded brilliantly."

Lee shivered. She wished he wouldn't touch her or look at her like that. It made her forget all her own warnings. It made her want to kiss him again. And she knew she couldn't. Once had been foolish. Twice would be like signing an order for her own self-destruction.

She moved her hand away from his to pick up another slice of pizza. Two was usually her limit. But if she used her hands for eating, he couldn't touch them. And she wouldn't lose her train of thought when he did.

The slightest hint of the woman who had mystified him had returned. Cody leaned back, studying her. "How long have you been doing cartoon voices?"

She shrugged, shifting so she could watch Sean. The slump of his shoulders told her that he had "died" again. He deposited another quarter into the machine. New lights appeared, declaring that he now had another ten lives to squander.

But she had only one, she thought. She couldn't shed any more tears. She had to remember that and not let this momentary aberration lull her into forgetting what she had been through and why.

"Forever, I think."

That sounded like something she'd say. "How did you get started?"

She watched Sean and silently cheered him on. Cody's question only vaguely registered. "Although it caught on when I was in school, it started when I pretended to be different people to keep myself company when I was a kid. I did a lot of flying back and forth between L.A. and Seattle." As an afterthought, she took a bite of the pizza slice. It was cold and chewy. She smiled disparagingly. "I did a lot of sitting in airports, too, waiting to be picked up."

He tried to picture her, small and alone. She stirred his sympathy. "By who?"

Lee abandoned the pizza and placed it back on her plate. "By whoever my parents sent to bring me back. They were divorced when I was twelve and got what I think is whimsically called 'joint custody.'" She had hated those years, hated the feeling that she wasn't really part of either parent's world because she was always flying to be with the other. "That's when two halves don't make a whole. Ever."

Lee stopped, suddenly realizing that she had said much more than she had intended to. She looked at her watch. "Um, it is getting late, Cody, and I do have to get up at an awful hour—"

He was just getting to know a little more about her. He didn't want her to go home yet. "Would you like that changed?"

She laughed and gave him a long, measured look. "Shouldn't you say something like 'Bibbidi-Bobbidi-Boo' before you grant a wish?"

"That's for fairy godmothers. General managers in charge of production don't have to say that when they change schedules." Was it his imagination, or was she retreating just a little? Why? He'd only offered to do her a favor. A perfectly normal one, he thought. Schedules did get revamped periodically, and why not to her advantage?

"My schedule's just fine," she said quickly. "I don't want anyone thinking that I'm taking advantage of the situation."

The smile on his lips was infinitely sexy. "You could try taking advantage of me."

She rose, picking up her purse. "I don't think anyone could take advantage of you, Cody Lancaster. You're far too formidable."

"I come with a marshmallow center."

She grinned. He was getting to her despite all her silent warnings about keeping a safe emotional distance between them. "That might be a useful piece of information to keep in mind."

Cody signaled to Sean as he rose from the bench. "C'mon, Sean. We have to get going." He crossed to the game and tapped the screen. "Wrap it up."

Sean looked up, disappointed as his father and Lee bracketed him on either side of the video game. "Awe, gee, Dad."

Cody nodded toward Lee. "Lee has to get up early for work."

Sean moved the joystick, and his character headed directly into the alien attack and dissolved instantly. "Okay." He turned from it as if it had never existed.

All Cody could do was shake his head as he gave Lee a side glance. "You really do work miracles, don't you?"

"It's in my contract. Under 'M.' Look it up." She linked her hand with Sean's and led the way across the sawdust-covered floor.

Cody followed, his footprints covering the ones made by Lee and Sean.

Though Lee offered a murmur of protest, Cody dropped Sean off at home with his housekeeper before taking Lee home. Sean pouted slightly as he stood in the driveway. He had wanted to come home with Lee and see Pussycat.

"Next time," Lee promised him in Sammy's voice. "We'll ditch the big guy—" she nodded at Cody "—and give you the run of the place."

"Okay." Sean's grin returned. He let Thelma hold his hand and he waved goodbye with his other one as his father pulled the car out of the driveway again.

Lee settled back in her seat and tried to tell herself that this wasn't a tinge of anxiety rippling through her. Or anticipation. She was just overtired. "Your housekeeper seems very nice."

"Thelma? Yes, she is."

He took a turn down a long, winding road. It seemed almost deserted this time of the evening except for an occasional car. He'd picked this route on purpose. He wanted to concentrate on the woman next to him, not on weaving in and out of heavy traffic.

"Thelma's been with me since I got married. She positively dotes on Sean. I always thought she had a way with him, but even she couldn't bring him around after Deborah died."

Lee heard the way his voice softened slightly when he mentioned his wife's name. She caught herself envying the woman, even though she was dead. He sounded as if he had really been in love with her. "Housekeepers aren't substitutes for parents, even the ones who dote." She thought of Anna, who always smelled of fresh-baked cookies. She had stayed on with Lee's mother after the divorce. Anna had tried very hard to make a difference for her when her parents had become wrapped up in their new lives. But it hadn't been the same.

Cody glanced at her for a moment. It was dark, and he couldn't see her expression. But she sounded sad and far away. "You sound like you speak from experience."

Lee looked down at her folded hands. "I do."

"Were you an only child?" he asked gently.

Lee shook off her mood and gave him a quizzical look. "Are we playing twenty questions?"

"No." Cody braked slowly as he came to a red light. "We're playing 'get to know your resident talented lady better.'"

There was that word again. *Your.* But she wasn't. She wasn't his or anyone's. And that was both the way she wanted it and hated it.

It's just a figure of speech, Lee, nothing more, she told herself.

"I had an older sister, Donna."

"Had?" Was she dead? Was that the cause of the sorrow that he saw in her eyes?

Silly, saying that, Lee thought. "I still have her." She shrugged. "But we were never close." Even though she had wanted to be. Donna had never seemed to have the time or the desire to be close. "She was a lot older and went her own way after the divorce. My parents', I mean," she added hurriedly.

Her postscript puzzled him. "What else could you mean?"

"Hers." Lee had almost said "mine," but she caught herself in time. That she was divorced wasn't even included in her personnel file at the station. She had checked "single" instead of "divorced" on her insurance application. Her marriage and divorce were nobody's business but her own.

He heard something in her voice, but wasn't sure what. "I take it that you're not very hot on the subject of marriage."

"Oh. I'm very hot on the subject of marriage." Lee shifted a little in her seat. Suddenly, she couldn't seem to get comfortable. "I only wish things like that were true, the way they are in those greeting-card commercials you see around the holidays. You know the ones, where Dad carves the turkey and Mom hugs everyone and blinks back tears." She turned away, looking out the side window. Dark shadows danced across the empty fields they passed. "I wanted a greeting-card family so bad I could taste it," she whispered, the words slipping out.

The wistfulness in her voice was almost palpable. "But they weren't," he guessed.

"No." Lee let out a sigh, reining herself in at the same time. "They weren't. Nobody's is."

He thought of his wife. "I'd like to think that mine was."

Lee turned to look at him, reeled in despite herself. "Your family?"

Cody thought of his big, blustering father and his regal-looking mother, who held the reins in the family but let his father believe otherwise. "Yes, them, too. But I was talking about my marriage. I was very, very happy." He banked down the feelings that were stirred. "We both were."

What would it have been like if she had been *his* wife instead of Lloyd's? Would those dreams she had always harbored actually have come true?

No, she knew better than that.

"I'm sorry. That it ended, I mean," she said quickly, "not that you were happy." She was tripping over her own tongue. She wished that Sean had come along with them. Then they couldn't have this conversation. And she wouldn't have had these longings stirred.

She wondered how much farther it was to her house. It was hard to gauge in the dark. She had never taken this road before, preferring cheery-looking stores lined up along the way to a long, lonely stretch of road.

"Why do I make you so nervous, Lee?" Cody had to know. "Do I remind you of someone?"

"No." She bit her lip. There was no harm in being honest. She didn't have to tell him everything. And there were things about Cody that did remind her of Lloyd. They were both tall and handsome, and their coloring was the same. As were other things too, probably. "Yes," she amended.

"Who?"

She should have known better than to answer a question for a man who didn't know when to stop pushing. "Someone." She shrugged, not looking at him. "Just someone."

It wasn't just "someone." It was a man who had meant something to her. Cody could tell from her voice. "Someone you didn't like?"

"No." A sad smile played on her lips as she remembered the beginning and the promises that had been there. Promises that had been empty. "Someone I liked very, very much. Once."

Cody waited, but Lee didn't continue. "But?"

Why did he have to know everything? Couldn't he just back off like everyone else did when she changed the subject? "He turned into someone I didn't know. Someone who was probably like that all along, but I just didn't see, because I was too young and too blind."

"Who?" A lover? He felt a wave of anger even though he knew no more than he had before. He knew he had no right to be angry, but he was. There was something standing between them, someone impeding any relationship that might be.

Lee turned and tried to sound casual. "I think your twenty questions are up."

He slowed to let another car pass. "Lee, I'd really like to know."

"Why?" They weren't going to have any sort of a relationship. She wasn't about to allow it. It would serve no purpose for him to have answers to his questions.

Cody didn't have a pat answer for that. Only a suspicion. One he didn't dare share with her. It concerned what there might be between them, what might grow if it was allowed. "That's what we have to find out. Together."

Together. What a powerful and frightening word. She couldn't let herself think about it. She'd been alone ever since she could remember. Even when she was married. "I don't think it's a wise idea."

He wasn't about to give up easily. "We won't know until we give it a chance."

"I know. I know already." Her voice gained in intensity as she tried to make him understand. "I'm not into commitments or relationships or—"

He wondered if she actually believed what she was saying. "This from a woman who single-handedly supports every charity in the country? I'd say that's a lot of commitment from someone who claims not to be 'into' commitments, wouldn't you?"

Slowly, he was stripping away her defenses, and she couldn't let him do that. "Are you filling in for Doctor John?" she asked, referring to a local radio station's popular talk show. "There are union rules about that, you know."

Maybe he had made enough headway for one night, he thought. But there would be other nights. Other opportunities. He wasn't going to stop until he had the full picture.

"Sorry." He pulled up into her in the driveway. "Will you have dinner with me again?"

She hadn't realized that they had arrived. Placing one hand on the car door handle, she started to get out. "Sure."

The answer sounded a touch too breezy. "Tomorrow night?"

She shook her head. "I have this charity event—"

He thought as much. "Wednesday?"

She wondered if he was going to go through all the days of the week. "Sorry. I've got a class at UCI. I'm sitting in."

She was wary. He could see it in her eyes. With only the moon as illumination, he still saw it. "We'll find a time."

Lee took a deep breath. "Sure. But I am kind of busy these next few—"

She was determined to put up a roadblock. He was just as determined to go through. "How about lunch?"

He could see he had caught her off guard. "At the studio. Sandwiches at high noon. With the door open."

She threw up her hands and laughed. "You don't give up, do you?"

"I wouldn't be here if I did."

She cocked her head. "Meaning?"

She'd given him a tiny bit of information about herself. He owed her a little about his own past. For him it was much easier to talk about. "I was a very typical poor little rich boy with absolutely everything handed to me."

"Lucky you."

"No, not really. It didn't prepare me for reality. What I really wanted most was a chance to see if I could make something of myself on my own."

"Well, that seemed to have turned out all right." From what she had seen at the studio, he was a lot more dynamic than the old production manager had been. She had to admit that things were running a lot more smoothly these days.

His expression changed slightly as he remembered. Nothing had prepared him for what had lain ahead. "I had a storybook life, a storybook marriage, and then everything blew up on me thirteen months ago. My wife died suddenly of something she shouldn't have in this day and age, and my perfect son withdrew and hardly talked to me."

Without thinking, Lee reached out and laid her hand on his.

Cody could almost feel the comfort radiating from her. He wondered if she knew just how much she had to give, how much she did give without even thinking about it. "It would have been very easy for me to fall into the party circuit and drink my way into oblivion.

But something kept me going." He turned to look at her. "I think that 'something' had you in mind."

Lee withdrew her hand, dropping it in her lap. "If it did, it was crazy. Cody, let's just be friends, okay?"

"A man can never have too many friends." But the look in Cody's eyes told Lee that he thought they were destined to be more than friends.

Well, he could think anything he wanted to, she told herself. As long as she kept her defenses up, everything was going to be fine.

But was it? Was it fine to always be on the outside yearning to break in? Wishing for love and all the trimmings?

Wishing for it and getting it were two entirely different things, and she knew it. The lesson had cost her dearly enough.

"Lee." He reached out to her.

She opened the door, ready to leave. "Yes?" Lee turned around to look at him.

He placed his hand over hers. "Don't bolt out of the car."

"Why not? I'm very good at bolting." But she stayed where she was.

"You're even better at other things."

"Video games."

Would she ever run out of obstacles to throw in his path? "At the moment, I was thinking of a particular kiss."

"Oh."

Her casual tone didn't fool him. "Don't tell me you weren't."

"I wasn't."

He moved closer, his hand on her shoulder. "You lie very poorly."

She was losing ground and she knew it. "Why, is my nose growing?"

"Lee?"

"What?"

"Can you stop talking for just a few minutes?"

She ran the tip of her tongue along her lower lip, her nerves jumping all through her. "I guess." She was almost trembling as he threaded his fingers through her hair and brought his lips to hers.

Instinctively, she dug her fingers into his shoulders. She had meant to move away, push away, stop him with a well-placed blow to the solar plexus. Instead, she was pulling him toward her, letting her head fall back as his kiss deepened and took her plunging to the place she had been to Saturday, painting it in colors even more vivid than before.

Somewhere in the distance, she could have sworn she heard taps playing. For her. But she didn't care. Like someone addicted, she clung to the feeling rushing through her, holding it dear, discounting the consequences she knew were inevitably to follow.

It was exactly as it had been before. A wild ride over the rapids. She pulled out all of his emotions from him, all of his feelings, and made him want her with an incredible urgency that he found overwhelming. If he didn't pull back now, he was going to take her here, now, and he knew that it was the worst thing that he could do to her. She was going to have to be coaxed, gently. She deserved it. Someone had treated her very, very badly, and though he was trying to find his way in the dark, Cody swore to himself that he was going to make it up to her.

"Lunch?" His breath came in snatches.

Lee blinked, trying to pull the world back into focus. "Is it noon already?"

He slid his hand over her cheek, trying not to laugh. Such a wonderfully funny, dear woman. "I meant tomorrow."

Right. She moved back. "Okay. You bring the sandwiches. Thelma's probably better at making them than I am."

This time he did laugh. "It just takes two pieces of bread."

She held up a finger. "Yes, but something has to go between them."

No one could be that bad when it came to preparing food. He wanted to say something to her, something to clear away the humor and let her know that she had come to be very important to him in an incredibly short period of time. And that it was going to be all right. But he knew that if he did, it would end right here, in the front seat of his car. And more than anything else in the world, Cody didn't want it to end. There were things he had to find out about her, things he had to find out about himself. And only she could show him.

"See you after your show," he called to her as she got out.

He stayed where he was, letting her walk to her front door by herself.

Chapter Eight

Cody was too good to be true.

Lee nodded as the director called a lunch break, and began looking around for her purse. And that was, she thought, the problem. Things that were too good to be true generally weren't. Lloyd had been "too good to be true," and life with him had turned into a nightmare of anguish. Lee liked Cody—a great deal, if she admitted it to herself, but not enough to separate her from her fears. Not enough to make her take a risk. It had happened once, what if it happened again? What if her judgment now was just as clouded, just as poor as it had been then?

She shouldn't be eating lunch with him. In order for her to hold her position, she knew that contact with Cody should be restricted to work alone. She didn't trust herself when she was around Cody. He had a way of making her forget everything else, a way of making her ignore all the danger signs she had so carefully

plotted. Allowing herself to be in his company was like
a recovering chocoholic surrounding herself with open
boxes of gourmet chocolate.

A wave of annoyance washed over her. Where was
her courage? Plenty of people ate and never plighted
their troth. The man didn't want to get serious, he
wanted to share a roast beef sandwich. Maybe a little
more, but certainly not anything serious. A harmless
flirtation. Nothing wrong with that.

It was just—just the way he looked at her, melting
everything inside of her that was solid and making her
wish—

Wishes were for the very young.

She leaned back and stretched, then saw Elyse looking at her through the large glass window that separated them in the recording booth. Lee knew that look.
Questions were dying to tumble out.

She might as well face them now instead of later, Lee
thought. Lee crossed the threshold of the booth, leaning casually against the doorjamb. "What?" she asked
Elyse. "You look as if you're going to explode if you
don't ask whatever it is that is rattling around in that
head of yours."

"Have you heard anything? About our jobs, I
mean," Elyse asked.

Lee shrugged. "Just what you already know. Looks
like he's going to keep us on." She looked at Elyse.
"Anything else you want to know?"

Elyse grinned. "Where do you stand with him? Cody,
that is."

Lee was surprised that she hadn't been attacked with
this question when she had walked in on Monday. Several of the people at the studio had been to the baseball

game on Saturday. Gossip was second only to breathing as an inalienable right at the station.

"Usually up to his shoulder, unless he's sitting, of course," Lee answered flippantly.

Elyse huffed, annoyed. "Stop making jokes, Lee."

"If I stop making jokes," Lee answered, the humor leaving her voice, "I'm going to be in big trouble."

The shorter woman gave her a knowing look. "Rings your chimes, huh?"

What was the point of denying that? And anyway, people could be enamored with one another with no strings or problems, right? It came under the heading of just one of those things. "Yes, he does. It feels as if I've got the Mormon Tabernacle Choir inside of me."

Elyse looked surprised at the admission. Surprised and delighted. "So what are you going to do about it?"

"Do?" Lee echoed, watching one of the technicians frown over the large spool of tape as he tried to get a sound just right. She shrugged. "Nothing. Enjoy it while it lasts, I suppose."

Elyse's red hair bobbed around her face as she shook her head in despair. "Lee, you've got to seize the moment. You've got to reel him in. You've got to—"

Lee pointed to Elyse's desk behind her. "You've got tracks to lay, remember?"

Elyse muttered something under her breath as she twisted around in her swivel chair and turned her attention to the technician who was softly swearing under his breath. "Here, it's this way," Elyse instructed.

Lee took her cue and left the booth, walking right into Jack Evans, who did the voice of Omar the Magnificent, Sammy Squirrel's nemesis. He acknowledged the brief contact with a grin that could have easily passed for a leer. "Hey, I heard that Lancaster gave you a ride home Saturday."

It must have made the evening news. "Yes, he did." She braced herself. Jack had been trying to get her to go out with him since she had come to work at the studio. Even if she had been so inclined, Jack's less than sterling reputation preceded him. Elyse had been the first to warn her that Jack subscribed to the braille system of socializing whenever possible.

A frown creased his perfect all-American looks. "What's he got that I haven't got?"

Lee smiled up sweetly. "Well, for one thing, he's a Homo sapien."

Elyse peered into the booth, grinning broadly. "Got you there, Jack."

Annoyed, the man stiffened. "Well, you know what they say about mixing business with pleasure."

"No." Lee couldn't resist baiting the man. "What *do* they say about mixing business with pleasure?"

Jack obviously hadn't been prepared to actually answer the rhetorical question. His smug expression slipped a notch. "Um, it's not good."

Lee nodded slowly, as if absorbing every nuance. "Very profound, Jack. Ever thought of writing a book of proverbs?" She swept her hands out before her, as if creating a scene. "It would be right up there with Confucius."

Jack brushed past Lee as he walked off the soundstage. "I've got new lines to go over."

"And a brain to find," Lee muttered to herself. Out of the corner of her eye, Lee saw Elyse trying to subdue a laugh.

Cody leaned back in his chair. He'd already temporarily shut off his phone. He had been busy all morning and he wanted a moment to think. Lee would be here for lunch soon and he wanted to gather his thoughts together.

He really hadn't thought that it could be possible. He remembered the day his heart broke, the day he had stood at the grave site and watched them lower Deborah's casket into the ground, sealing her away from him. He remembered hearing Thelma crying softly behind him, Sean holding on to him tightly. He remembered the feel of the tears on his face. The sun had been shining and he had told Sean that the angels were smiling as they were taking Mommy home with them. He had gone completely numb inside. The magic had gone out of his life. And at that moment, he had known that he could never really care about another woman again.

Deborah had been gone for a little more than a year. It didn't seem right that he should be drawn to someone else so soon.

And yet, in his heart, Cody knew that Deborah would have wanted this for him. Part of the reason he had loved her as much as he had was because she had been so selfless. She wouldn't have wanted him and Sean to spend the rest of their lives mourning. His sister wrote to him weekly, urging him to get back into the mainstream again. In Sara's last letter she had included an article that said people who had been happily married tended to remarry more often and more quickly after the loss of a spouse than the ones who had suffered through a bad relationship....

He paused, the words he had read last night suddenly sinking in with new meaning.

Was that it? Had Lee had a bad relationship? Or a bad marriage? Was that what was making her so skittish each time he drew near? Was she afraid of *getting* close?

He felt that there was something there between them, both good and bad. The bad had nothing to do with him. It was the way she looked at him at times, as if appraising him, weighing him against someone else.

The someone she had mentioned last night. Someone she had said she thought she knew but hadn't.

He flipped open her file and looked down at her photo. She was funny and flippant one moment, incredibly seductive the next. Lighthearted whirlwind. Sexy lady. Hurt woman. Which was the real Leanne Sheridan? He had a feeling it was all of the above.

Lee walked down the narrow hallway to Cody's office. She had absolutely no idea why she was doing this to herself. It wasn't a test. If it was a test, she already knew she was flunking it miserably. All her bravado from an hour ago was gone. Lunches *did* count. She *wanted* to be in his company, felt drawn to him like the proverbial moth to the flame.

Her choice of simile alone should have warned her, she thought. She was in for pain and heartache. That's all that ever happened to the moth. It singed its wings, just as she had singed hers when she had run headlong into what she had hoped was happiness.

Why couldn't she learn? She was both afraid of breaking and yearning so hard to break the barriers around her that held her back. Afraid to try, afraid not to. No matter what, she was still that little girl who had watched her parents' marriage break up, wanting the warmth she felt was due to her. Still that young woman who thought she had found love, only to have it turn into bitter disappointment.

All the time and effort she volunteered to charities should have been enough to satisfy her needs, and yet it wasn't. She still hungered for something more, something she knew couldn't be hers. Just one some-one to build her life around, someone who would want to build his life around her. Someone to love who would love her in return.

But it wasn't meant to happen.

She peered into Cody's office, deciding that maybe it was for the best if she took a rain check. A long rain check. "Cody, I'm—"

He second-guessed her. He was on his feet and at the door the moment he saw a glimmer of her silver blond hair. "Hungry, I hope." Gently, he took her hand and drew her into the room.

No had always been a difficult word for her to say. "Well, actually..."

He was leading her to his desk. With his work cleared off to one side, his desk looked like a mahogany picnic table. He had thrown down a tablecloth and set up plates and glasses for two. The sandwiches were not in a sack. Thelma had packed everything in a basket to add to the romantic ambience.

"Everything but the ants," Lee murmured, tickled that he had gone to such trouble.

"Those can be brought in from outside," he of-fered. Lee made a face. "Thelma packed three kinds of sandwiches." He took them out and spread the wrapped packages before her. "She wasn't sure what you'd like."

Lee picked one up and pulled out a corner of the wrapping. Ham and Swiss. "Is she always so eager to please?"

He poured a little white wine into a glass and placed it before her. "She got a little excited when I mentioned that the picnic included you. She thinks we're dating."

Lee raised her eyebrows. "Did you tell her that we're only chewing?"

Cody poured himself a glass of wine, then gestured Lee to sit in the chair next to his. "Thelma is an old-fashioned British romantic and easily crushed. I'm still trying to find a way to break it to her. In the meantime, I thought I'd let her hang on to her dreams. Besides, this *could* be considered a date."

She usually didn't drink anything stronger than ginger ale until after five. Today, she thought she might need a little something extra. Lee took a long sip of her wine before she asked, "By whom?"

"Anyone." Cody handed her a napkin and eyed her as she took it. "You, maybe."

Slowly, she took a bite of her sandwich and chewed thoughtfully. This was hard, but she was going to have to stop it before it went too far. And took her with it. "Cody, it's not that I don't like you."

He didn't have an iota of interest in the sandwich he was eating. It might have been a mud pie for all that he noticed. "Encouraging."

She turned around and sighed, dragging a hand through her hair. The sandwich, forgotten, was in her other hand. "I *can't* like you."

He watched her. It was incredible how she managed to change right before his very eyes. One second she was confident, the next moment appealingly vulnerable. He found himself falling for all her facets. "Sure you can. It's not that hard."

"Yes, it is," she insisted. "If I like you, if I really let myself like you, it'll be incredibly hard." *On me.*

He took her hand across the table and held it. "You're not involved with anyone."

She wanted to pull it away, but just for a moment she let the warmth of his touch reach her. "No, and I don't want to be."

"Why?"

Now she pulled her hand away. "That's my business." The frost she tried to put into her voice didn't quite make it.

He wasn't going to be put off that easily. "You've fed me cookies and let me touch your battery terminals. I think that makes it my business." Taking a page out of her book, he raised and lowered his eyebrows comically, doing the worst impression of Groucho Marx she had ever seen. "Unless you let everyone touch your battery terminals."

She laughed. She couldn't help herself. Some of the tension shooting through her body went temporarily on hold. "You've got to stop being so likable."

He leaned his head on his upturned hand, teasing her with his eyes. "Why?"

She let out a breath like a gust of wind. "Because you're making it hard for me."

He nodded his head. "Good."

Restless, feeling hemmed in by herself as much as by him, Lee rose and moved toward the window. "No, not good."

Cody went to stand behind her. He placed his hands on her shoulders lightly. "Tell me about it, Lee."

There was a sea of cars outside the window. Beyond that, a murky sky. Smog was bad today. There was nothing to look at. "No. Maybe. Someday."

He turned her around gently and looked at her face. "Is this Morse code?"

She laughed depreciatively. "If it were, I'd be sending out SOS signals."

He wanted to kiss her, to hold her, to make all the pain he saw in her eyes fade away. "I'm the only one here to intercept them."

She raised her chin, as if resigning herself to something. "Then I guess I'm sunk."

"Looks that way." But they weren't talking about the same end result. He could see that. What had happened to her before she had walked into his life? "Were you married before, Lee?"

He wasn't going to let this go until she gave him an answer, she thought, but instinctively, she hedged anyway. "Before what?"

He dug deep for patience. "Before this minute."

Because he held her, she couldn't turn away. But she lowered her eyes. "Yes."

"Is that why you look at me the way you do?"

Her head snapped up. "How do I look at you?" She had thought that she was keeping it all locked inside. Apparently not.

He cupped her cheek, wishing she would trust him. "Like a doe caught in the headlights of an oncoming car."

It wasn't a favorable image. She didn't like to think of herself in those terms. She would have liked to believe that she was up to facing anything. And that no one could detect the vulnerability that existed inside. "Yes, and I don't want to go 'splat' again."

She had to leave before other things were said. Before she told him everything and laid herself bare. Before she cried.

"Look—" Lee pulled away from him "—I just remembered, I don't eat lunch." She was backing out the door. "I—"

He knew he had to let her go, at least for now. But he took her hand for only a moment. "Lee, whoever he was, *whatever* he was, I'm not him."

Lee looked into his eyes and something stirred inside. If she were free to love, if she *could* love, it should have been this man. But it was too late for dreams like that. "I know that."

"Then don't condemn me because of him." More than anything else, Cody wanted to slam the door shut, to make her stay here. But he knew that it would have been the worst thing he could do. He could only talk to her and hope that she would come around. He let go of her hand. "God knows, I've got enough faults of my own. I don't need to carry around another man's baggage."

Lee turned, then stopped. What was she doing? She was fleeing, like a coward, like something she hated. He was only trying to be nice. And as long as she didn't let her feelings get out of hand, it would be all right.

"Okay." Lee stepped back inside and let the door close behind her.

"Okay?" For a minute, Cody could only stare at her in confusion.

Nonchalantly, as if nothing had happened, Lee crossed back to the desk and picked up her sandwich. "Maybe I will eat a sandwich."

"Fine." He returned to his desk. When she had said she liked to keep people guessing, he had never dreamed that she could be this good at it.

He was going to have to tread very lightly if he was going to tread at all. Someone, probably her ex-husband, Cody surmised, had hurt her very much. Someday he was going to get her to the point where she trusted him enough to tell him about it. Right now, he didn't want to scare her out of his life.

Though it was difficult, he reined in his fast-flowering feelings for her and his need to be with her again, alone. He played dirty. Because he knew how crazy the boy was about her, he used Sean.

"He misses you," he told her, cornering her just as Lee was about to fly out the door to her cartoon taping.

"And I miss him." And she did. She had grown attached to Sean in a very short time. But then, she always was a pushover for children. And Sean was adorable.

She knew it wasn't going to end here. Cody had something more on his mind. She could tell by the way he blocked her exit.

"Why don't I bring you over to the house later on today, after you finish helping Sammy store nuts for the winter?"

She laughed at the way he summarized her work. As a matter of fact, this week's story did have to do with storing nuts. It was a takeoff on the story of the grasshopper and the ants, with Sammy playing the ants and Shadoe being a lovable grasshopper.

"I can drive myself." She was playing devil's advocate on purpose, seeing what he would answer.

"Yes, but taking two cars to the restaurant can get cumbersome."

She looked at him. He was going a little fast for her. So, what else was new, she thought. "What restaurant?"

"The one I'm taking you to tonight, after your visit with Sean," Cody informed her, copying the innocent tone she had used with him on occasion.

Lee crossed her arms in front of her and gave him a penetrating look that was supposed to make him flinch. It didn't. "Just like that?"

"No, I'm giving you about six hours to come up with an excuse."

"Which you won't listen to."

"Which I won't listen to," he agreed, slipping an arm around her shoulders. Lightly, he placed a kiss on her temple. The intimate gesture created a flurry of activity within the pit of her stomach. "One of the things I like best about you is that you catch on incredibly fast."

Lee stepped back. "Cody, it won't work, this—" she spread her hands wide, helplessly "—this 'dating' business," she cried for lack of a better word.

"Let me worry about that. You just concentrate on 'chewing.' Deal?"

For now, she surrendered. She turned slightly and saw Elyse watching them. "Do I have a choice?"

Cody grinned. "No."

"Deal." It wasn't so hard to agree. Just dinner. Nothing more.

"I'll pick you up at five."

She was walking off a plank and she knew it, but she was enjoying it. She probably needed to have her head examined.

When Cody brought Lee into the house that evening, Sean was overjoyed to see her. Instantly, he dragged her off to his room to show her all the things that were important to him. Cody hung back, letting Sean monopolize Lee before he took her off to dinner.

Cody knew that in his own way, his son was as crazy about Lee as he was growing to be. She wasn't filling the hole that Deborah had left behind for them. No one could do that. But Lee was certainly filling their lives in her own unique way.

When it came time for Lee and his father to leave, Sean reluctantly followed her down the stairs to the front door. "You'll be back soon?" he asked.

Impulsively, she kissed Sean. "Very soon."

"We'll both hold you to that," Cody whispered in her ear as he took her arm.

She was tightening the trap herself, she thought. And willingly. What was the matter with her? When would she learn?

Maybe later.

She turned and waved to the boy. Thelma stood behind Sean, one thin, fine-boned hand protectively on his shoulder. "Stay out as long as you like, Mr. Lancaster." The genial smile went from ear to ear on the porcelain face. "Sean will be just fine."

Cody held the door open for Lee as she slid into the passenger side. "I think she's just given permission for me to stay out all night."

Lee smoothed her skirt down before she looked up at him. "You'll get lonely by yourself. I have to be in early. I have this slave driver as a boss who insists on my working these ungodly hours."

Cody laughed as he came around the front of the car and got in. "I told you that could be changed. I could move the taping up."

"I don't want preferential treatment."

He started the car, then looked at her before he backed out of the driveway. "What do you want, Lee?"

She shrugged, keeping her voice light. "Something that doesn't exist." Then, giving him a flash of the grin that was beginning to haunt his dreams, she added, "A boss that doesn't ask five thousand questions."

The restaurant he had chosen was intimate, charming and close by. "I'm not your boss tonight."

"All right," she amended. "A date that doesn't ask five thousand questions."

Traffic was progressing at a steady pace. He glanced at her and raised one brow. "Date?"

She knew he'd catch that as soon as it had come out. "Slip of the tongue."

The smile on his lips was one of self-satisfaction. "Maybe I'm wearing you down."

"You're certainly wearing me out," she said, willing to concede. Quickly, she changed topics. "Where are we going?"

He switched into the right lane. "To a restaurant with candlelight and soft music."

She should have guessed. He was really playing dirty. "No food?"

"And food."

"I kind of liked pizza and video games and sawdust." At least there she could divert him.

"I know, but I want to look at you without children running up and asking you to demonstrate your prowess at the games."

For the moment, she told herself to relax and enjoy this. After all, it *was* a public place. And he was awfully sweet. "You probably don't play well."

"No," he admitted, "I don't."

"I could teach you."

"I bet you could." His voice softened. There was a lot she could teach him. She had already taught him that he still believed in magic, still believed in happiness. And perhaps there were a few things that he could teach her. "You've already taught me to laugh."

"I thought you did that pretty naturally on your own."

"Not since my wife died."

Lee found herself wondering what Deborah Lancaster had been like. And how she measured up against her. "She must have been pretty special."

"Yes." But he didn't want to talk about the past, not tonight. He wanted to talk about the present. "And so are you."

Compliments always embarrassed her. "Not everyone can do twenty-five different voices."

He brought the car to a halt before a small restaurant located a short distance from the pier. In the distance, sea gulls called to one another. "I'm not talking about your cartoon repertoire." He got out and then opened the door for her. "There are a lot of other things that are special about you."

A memory flashed through her mind as she got out. Lloyd standing over her, telling her how special she was, and then, not that much later, telling her how stupid she was, how she could never do anything right. She winced involuntarily.

"What's the matter?"

"Nothing." She shook her head, as if to rid herself of the memory. "Just a chill."

Cody placed his arm around her shoulders as they walked to the restaurant. She looked up at him, something unreadable in her eyes. "I just want to keep the chill away from you, Lee."

And what would keep it away from her heart when it struck there? More than anything in the world, she wanted to believe him. But she had believed Lloyd with all her heart when he had told her that he loved her and would take care of her. And it had all been lies.

For tonight, she pushed the memory aside. Cody deserved better and she was going to try to give it to him. But just for tonight.

mention it before? Surely that was what he would
tell her. Surely it was best anyway, that he would need
would fire carefully. And it was up to him to
For tonight she had had his cautious tease. Odd, she
was no better and her was going to have to give it up. Just
not past her tonight.

Chapter Nine

Looking back, Cody had to admit that it had been one
of the most interesting evenings in his life. The food had
been excellent, the wine perfect, the ambience subtly
romantic. And the company—the company had been
the best part. It had been amusing, warm, sexy. In a
word, he thought, incredible. In a shorter word, it had
been Lee. That, he knew, summed it up neatly.

He sat back on her gray-blue sofa, letting the soft
Italian leather mold itself around his body like a gloved
hand. He felt content, as if his life was finally taking
shape, as if he was finally doing more than just surviv-
ing and going through the motions of living.

"Could you sit down for a second?" He turned his
head as she disappeared behind him. "You're making
me dizzy."

Lee moved around the living room, straightening
things. There was this charged energy coursing through
her that sought release. She looked over her shoulder at

him. "Is that the same thing as sweeping you off your feet?"

She wished she could calm down. It was as if there were this little hamster running around on a wheel inside of her and he had gone berserk. There seemed to be no way to calm down.

As she walked past him again, Cody took hold of her hands and forced her to sit next to him. "Can we be serious here for a minute, Lee?"

Lee summoned courage from somewhere. "I'd really rather not."

He had anticipated her response. It didn't stop him. Cody wanted her to be at ease with him. He wanted to make her understand. Maybe if he put it in terms she could relate to. "Lee, you make me feel like I'm Gene Kelly and I want to go out jumping from puddle to puddle, singing at the top of my lungs and waking up the neighbors."

"I don't think my neighbors would like that." She tried to get up. The grip on her hands was gentle, but firm. She stayed sitting next to him.

He saw the wary flash in her eyes. He didn't want to make her uncomfortable. For a second, he debated forgetting this for now. But if he did, he knew they'd never get over this "thing" between them, never get any further than they were right now.

"You've been moving around all evening like the proverbial cat on a hot tin roof." Slowly, he moved his hands up along her arms, resting them on her shoulders. He felt the tension receding from her body. "Why don't you relax? Just be yourself."

Lee tried to concentrate on something other than the fact that he was touching her, other than the fact that she wanted him to. "This is myself."

"No, I don't think so." Using only one hand, the other still on her shoulder, he slowly played along the planes of her face. "This isn't what you're like when Sean's around."

She tried to draw away and found she couldn't. "I thought you found *that* me boring." Her voice almost cracked as she said it. What was he doing to her? With just a look, with just the slightest touch, he was melting her bones like some kind of irresistible infrared laser beam.

"Boring?" Lightly, his fingers feathered along her brow, her temples, cheekbones. "Since when is a tornado boring? I've never met anyone as exciting as you, Lee, as funny, bright, warm."

Lee's breath caught in her lungs and refused to move. It seemed to happen a lot around him. "Yes, I am definitely getting warm here."

Cody leaned toward her, her face framed in his palms. "I won't hurt you, Lee."

Yes, you will.

The words echoed in her mind, but she left them unsaid. As his lips drew near, swiftly blotting out everything else in her head, Lee still tried to tell herself that she could be blasé about all this. That "love" was only a four-letter word in a dictionary instead of something that she had once so desperately quested after and failed so miserably at attaining.

But she was a big girl now, a lot older than the nineteen-year-old student who had had stars in her eyes when she blindly entered into a disastrous marriage. She could handle this situation. She could handle anything.

No, she couldn't.

All bets were off, and she knew it as soon as his lips touched hers. For now, for this one moment, she wouldn't think of what was to come. She would only think of now. And maybe, somehow, that would be enough.

It was all she would ever have.

Lee wrapped her arms around Cody's neck as his lips caused heaven to explode within her, showering her with rainbows and flowers that spun around her. Or maybe she was doing the spinning. Everything tightened within her as yearning sprang, full-grown and demanding, throughout her body.

Cody wanted to touch her everywhere, to possess her. He slid his hands languidly along her body, molding her to him, assuring himself that she was real and not just someone who, in his neediness, he had made up. She felt so good, so soft. Urges slammed through him like thunder, making him want to make love to her here, on this sofa that seemed created to absorb them. He wanted to make love with her now and for the rest of his life.

He forced himself to hold back. Whatever there was in her past, it wasn't a small matter, not to Lee. He didn't want to frighten her away. She had become too important to him. He couldn't risk losing her because of his own demanding needs. Hers had to come first, even if it cost him. And it did.

Murmuring her name softly, he pressed his lips to her neck. Lee felt everything swirling around her. The world had been swallowed up in soft cotton. And the cotton was on fire. It had been so long, so very long since anyone had held her like this, had wanted her like this. And he was so incredibly gentle. He wasn't pulling at her, demanding his 'due.'

He made her want to cry.

Damn, she was going to melt right here and now, into his arms like drawn butter.

And the worst of it was, she didn't care. She wanted him, wanted to make love with him, wanted to feel his body against hers. Her body ached for him. *She* ached for him.

Lee let her fingers tangle in his hair, only half-aware of what she was doing. Every ounce of concentration was dissolved even as she desperately sought to anchor herself to earth.

What, oh what, was he doing to her?

He was making her crazy, that's what he was doing.

Her blouse had pulled free of her skirt, and Cody was slowly inching his hands up along her quivering skin, leisurely, gently, as if his heart wasn't hammering with each movement. He could feel her heart beneath his fingertips now as he caressed her breast. It was beating hard, beating that way because of him. Cody covered her mouth with his own again as he felt her gasp and then tighten her hold on his shoulders.

He stripped her of all her defenses, reducing her to a mass of needs and passions that flamed high. Gone were all the mannerisms, the flippant humor that she used as her shield. There was no shield left to protect her. There was only her. And she was frightened and vulnerable, but oh, if he drew away now, if he turned away, she would plummet down, shattered.

The shrill ringing behind her made Lee jump, a scream stifled in her throat. She looked around, dazed and disoriented.

"What—?"

One more moment and there would have been no room for restraint, no room for common sense. With effort, Cody moved away, his arms still around her. His breathing was labored as he tried to steady it. "I think that's the phone."

"Phone?" she repeated dumbly. "Oh, the phone."

Lee pulled her blouse into place. How was she ever going to pull the rest of herself into place? she wondered, still partially dazed. "I'd better answer it." Her voice sounded hoarse, strained to her ear. Small wonder. "It might be important."

Cody felt something akin to sadness seeping in as he watched the slightly dazed look in her eyes fading. "I could offer to rip it out of the wall."

She laughed, clinging to the opportunity to make small talk. "I'd only have to have someone come to put it back in." Turning, she reached for the telephone on the long table behind the sofa and brought the receiver to her ear. "Hello?"

"Lee?" a little, uncertain voice asked.

Small world. "Hello, Sean." She settled back against the sofa and glanced at her watch. It was nearly ten. She saw Cody staring at her. "Shouldn't you be asleep?"

"Sean?" Cody echoed. What was Sean doing calling at this hour? And how did he get her number? "My Sean?"

Lee covered the receiver. "None other. I gave him my number in case he wanted to talk to Sammy some time," she added to answer the perplexed expression on his face. Lee pressed the speakerphone so that Cody could listen in on the conversation. "What's up, Sean?"

"Lee," the small voice quavered, "there're monsters in my room."

"Yes, there're some in mine, too." She grinned at Cody as she twisted the long cord around her finger.

"Really?" Sean breathed, his voice half excited, half leery. "What are you doing with them?"

"There's just one," Lee clarified, still looking at Cody. *And he's going to be my undoing if I'm not careful,* she added silently.

Cody leaned forward so that his voice could carry. "She bit him."

"Dad?" Sean sounded confused. "Are you there, too?"

"Yes, Sean. I'm here. I'm helping Lee get rid of her monster."

No you're not, Lee thought. *Not by a long shot.*

"Can you come home and get rid of mine?" Sean asked, his voice hopeful. "Thelma's no help," he moaned. "She's asleep."

"Sean, is Sammy in your room?" Lee asked, suddenly inspired.

"Yeah."

"Well, put him at the foot of your bed. He'll guard you. No monster's going to mess with Sammy Squirrel."

Where did she get all this? Cody wondered, marveling at her imagination.

"For sure?" Sean asked.

"For sure," Lee promised.

"Can you stay on the phone until I get him?"

She could hear the worry in his voice as he asked her to wait. "I'll be here as long as it takes."

"You really are a very special lady," Cody said softly as they heard Sean put down the phone and go down the hallway to his room.

"I seem to have this fatal attraction for people under four feet."

"And over," Cody told her as he reached out to stroke her cheek. He felt a nerve quiver beneath his fingers. "I'm almost six-two."

"He's there!" Sean announced proudly.

"You're safe now," Lee told him.

"I'll be home as soon as I can, son," Cody added.

The voice that answered sounded a good deal more confident. "You don't have to hurry anymore, Dad. 'Bye, Lee. And thanks."

"Anytime, Sean. 'Bye." She hung up, breaking the connection. For a moment, there was nothing but silence in the room.

The moment gone, it was time to leave. Cody rose to his feet. Feeling a reluctance in her limbs, Lee rose as well. "Well, I guess I'd better go home."

"Yes, I guess you'd better." Before I do something stupid again, she thought.

But he didn't want to leave. It was as if his shoes had been glued to the floor. "Lee."

She steeled herself. She wasn't going to be any good to herself, ever, if she caved in now. "Cody, I don't want anything happening between us."

"Too late." He shook his head, his eyes gliding along her lips. "It's already happening."

Lee took a step back. She felt as if he had physically touched her. "No."

He held her in place with just a look. "Are you going to tell me that you didn't feel anything just then?"

"No, I didn't." She felt desperation mounting. *Please, I can't go through this again, I can't go into a relationship, wanting. It's not going to happen.*

He raised her chin until he could see her eyes. "Honestly."

She sighed. Pretending was her gift. But not lying. "Yes, I felt something."

Why was she so afraid? Why wouldn't she trust him? "Don't make it sound like a death warrant."

Because she suddenly needed the contact, she placed her hands on his arms. "It is, for me. Cody, I've been through this before."

"So have I." Although not quite this intense this fast, he thought. "Obviously we didn't arrive at the same end results." He wanted to take her into his arms, to make all the hurt go away. But he knew that she wasn't a child and that that wouldn't be nearly enough. She needed more. "How long were you married, Lee?"

She tried to smile and only half succeeded. "Long enough to know I'm not any good at it."

He couldn't accept that. How could she? "Did it ever occur to you that it might have been his fault and not yours?"

"Sure," she said a little too quickly. But it had been her fault for staying in a destructive relationship. Her fault for being weak. She was never going to be weak again. "That doesn't change anything." She let her hands drop and crossed toward the door. "You go in with dreams, you come out with confetti."

Taking hold of her shoulder, he turned Lee around to face him. "It doesn't have to be that way."

Lee stayed firm. She had to be. It was a matter of survival. "I can't chance it. The risk is too great."

"Give *me* a chance, Lee. We'll take it slow, one step at a time. And we'll both see. All right?"

She took a deep breath. She knew he wasn't about to go until she agreed. "All right."

Who knew? Maybe in time . . .

"Now you'd better go." She made an attempt to playfully push him out the door. "Your son's waiting for you."

"Sammy's with him, remember?" Cody took her into his arms again.

Funny how she could pretend to be safe there. The key word, she knew, was pretend. And then he kissed her and she wasn't safe anymore. The kiss was almost savagely passionate, as if he could trust himself to kiss her that way only when he was leaving.

"One more like that," he whispered against her hair, "and I might not be able to go."

Lee leaned her head against his chest, her heart pounding so hard that it physically hurt. "One more like that and I might not let you go."

Cody raised her head with the tip of his finger under her chin. "See, one step at a time."

She laughed as she shook her head. "That was some step. It was at thirty-thousand feet with no ground under it." She sighed. "I can't seem to think when you kiss me."

He smiled into her eyes. "That's the whole idea. You're not supposed to think, Lee." Lightly, Cody touched his lips to hers one more time. "You're just supposed to feel."

And then he slipped out the door. She leaned against it, as much for support as to close it. "That's the whole problem, Cody," she whispered to the door. "I do. And I know exactly where it's going to get me."

It wasn't going to be easy, Cody thought as he glanced over his shoulder at the light burning in her living room window. But it wasn't impossible. She cared about him. That much was evident, and he cared about her. More than he thought possible. She was warm, witty and thoroughly lovable. And there was a core of passion that he had tapped into and meant to tap into again. On a permanent basis, if he didn't miss his guess.

The lady, he decided as he got into his car and turned it on, wasn't going to know what hit her when he was through. Two could play at this tornado game.

Over the next six weeks Cody slowly laid siege to Lee, and she slipped into his trap without fully realizing what was happening. Or, if she subconsciously knew, she was blocking it out and pretending she didn't. Her only line of defense was to quickly change the subject whenever things became too serious, whenever Cody seemed inclined to pursue the subject of the future.

But to all intents and purposes, Lee let herself go, enjoying everything that being with Cody had to offer. While she was with him, she could almost believe that things she had once dreamed about were true. That a man and a woman could get along, could fit together like two pieces of a jigsaw puzzle. That those greeting-card commercials she was such a sucker for had more than a ghost of truth in them. But each time she felt herself being drawn into thinking that just maybe, it might work, she reminded herself that this was the 'before' stage. Before commitment, before marriage. She had had a wonderful time with Lloyd, too. Before. Afterward, it had been another matter. Another world. The real one.

Lee told herself that because she refused to let Cody even raise the word *commitment,* everything was going to be all right and she wasn't going to get hurt. They could just go on dating for the next thirty or forty years.

She could feel that what there was between Cody and her was something very, very nice, passionate yet warm.

But she knew that it would all be ruined if she allowed herself to actually believe that they had a future together.

Cody hoped that her reluctance to discuss her marriage would fade. In the meantime, he simply enjoyed the time they spent together. They alternated between going out alone and taking Sean along with them. When Sean was included, entertainment tended to lean toward amusement parks.

"I don't know who's enjoying this more, Sean or you." Cody found an unoccupied bench and sat down. Sean collapsed next to him, clutching the dinosaur that Lee had won for him at the bottle knock-down. Lee settled in next to them, finishing the last of her hot dog.

"It's probably a toss-up." Lee wiped her fingers on a napkin and stuffed it into her purse. "I never got to do this kind of stuff as a kid."

Cody leaned back on the bench, studying her. Another piece of the puzzle, he thought. "Your parents didn't have the money?"

"They didn't have the time." She leaned over and zipped up Sean's Windbreaker. Evenings had started getting chilly. She could smell the crispness in the air. Christmas wasn't all that far away, she mused. Without realizing it, excitement began to build at the thought. "My dad was a bank president, my mother, a college professor." She shrugged carelessly. After all these years, it shouldn't bother her. But it always did, just a little. "They were wrapped up in their separate worlds, always busy."

He could see that it still hurt. "I'm sorry."

She smiled quickly, shoving her hands into her jacket pockets to keep them warm. "Oh, it wasn't such a bad childhood. No one beat me."

He wondered at the strange expression on her face when she said that. *Had* someone raised a hand to her? Her ex? "Maybe not physically," he said tentatively, waiting for her to continue.

But she didn't want to talk about it. She had had too nice a time today. "Don't turn philosophical on me, Cody. I'm much too sleepy to hold my own."

He laughed. "That'll be the day. You, lady, could hold your own *in* your sleep." Leaning over Sean, who was slumped against him, Cody kissed her lightly, subtly arousing the passion that laid just beyond.

It was a warm, comfortable feeling, with desire only a heartbeat away. It was a feeling that she promised herself she wouldn't allow to become commonplace. If she did, she'd miss it much too much once it was gone.

But for now, just for now, she'd let herself like it. Maybe it wouldn't do too much harm.

She tapped Cody on the shoulder and then pointed to Sean. His eyes were closed, even though his hands were tightly wrapped around his new prize. "I think we've lost him."

Cody lifted Sean up into his arms. The boy murmured something inaudible and curled up against his father's chest.

Lee brushed Sean's hair away from his face. "He feels a little warm to me." She frowned, looking at the small sleeping face. "Maybe it was all this excitement."

Cody nodded. "Probably. That and four hot dogs. Time to go home, anyway," he agreed. He began to lead the way out of the park, to his car. He glanced at Lee walking next to him. "Can I interest you in spending the night?"

She was tempted, sorely tempted, but giving herself to him would be breaking down her final barrier. She'd have nothing left to fight with. Once she gave herself to him, once she made love with him, she would be committed. And it would be the beginning of the end.

"Cody, don't spoil the day."

"That wasn't what I had in mind."

It was hard holding on to his patience, hard when he wanted her in his arms, in his bed. In his life, permanently. He knew he had promised himself to go slowly, but it was draining him. He wanted her so badly that at times it kept him awake at night. He'd lie there, just thinking about her. Aching for her. Some men went through life never knowing what love was. He had been lucky enough to fall in love twice, to have magic touch him twice. He wasn't about to let her go. Not when he knew in his heart that she felt the same.

But how could he overcome her demons when she wouldn't even talk to him about them? About her marriage. That was the key to it, and she refused to let him have it.

He had to go away on business tomorrow morning. But they were going to have it out when he returned, he promised himself.

"This is your last opportunity to take advantage of me for a week," he told her as they reached his car. "I'm leaving tomorrow."

She'd forgotten about that. Seven days without him. It should have made her feel relieved. No subtle pressure, no one to mentally fight off. But it only made her feel sad.

It was a warning of things to come, she told herself.

"We'll talk when you get back." She tried to sound cheery as she opened the door for him.

Cody gently placed Sean on the back seat and buckled the sleeping boy in. "Yes," Cody glanced at her over his shoulder, "we will."

Lee got in on the passenger side and stared out the window. It was a clear night. The stars were out, winking like tiny pinpricks on a blanket of black velvet. She picked one star out and kept it in her sight as Cody drove her home. If she believed in things like wishing stars, she would have made a wish right now, a wish that her life would have begun the day she met Cody. Then she would be able to love him the way he should be loved.

For then there would be no fear of failure.

No, she corrected herself, not fear, *knowledge* of failure. And that single word made all the difference in the world.

Chapter Ten

Cody had the taxicab driver drop him off at the studio and wait before he made his way to the airport. There were documents to pick up that he had left behind. But the real reason he was there was to see Lee one more time before he left for Denver. He was behaving like a schoolboy—and he loved it. It felt wonderful to be in love again.

She was on the soundstage, waiting for the technicians to set up for the next take, when Cody passed. He looked in, waved and winked, then continued on to his office, hoping that she'd find a way to follow him.

Lee drummed her fingers on the cover of the script. She had a job to do. She was being paid to do Princess Enchantra today, as well as the Queen Mother. But Cody would be gone for a week. She bit her lower lip and looked over toward Elyse. "How long before you're ready to tape?" she called.

Elyse grinned. "You've got enough time for a long farewell kiss if you hustle." Lee dropped the script on a canvas-back chair and hurried past the sound booth. "Do I get to go to the wedding?" Elyse called after Lee.

"You get to go to any wedding you want, Elyse," Lee said over her shoulder. "It's a free country."

When she reached his office, Cody was snapping his briefcase shut. She ran her hands up her arms. Why did that small action seem so final to her? It was just a business trip.

"Here to send me off?" he asked, turning around. He had sensed her presence even without looking. Her light perfume wafted through the air, surrounding him, arousing him. He wondered if anyone else was aroused by the scent of wildflowers.

"A committee of one." She spread her hands wide as if to call attention to herself. Then her expression sobered just a little. "How long did you say you'd be gone?" Maybe she had misunderstood. Maybe it wasn't for seven days. Why did it seem like an eternity?

Abandoning his briefcase, he placed his hands on her waist. "A week."

Each time he touched her, Lee found that there was less energy left to draw on with which to resist. "I hear the snow bunnies are in season now. It's November."

Gently, he pressed her against him until there wasn't enough room for a prayer. "I know what month it is and I'm not interested in a snow bunny. I have my eye on a particular squirrel."

She tried to keep the smile from her lips, but it lingered in the corners of her mouth. "I think Sean's got dibs on Sammy."

"That's okay." He kissed her forehead, and then each one of her eyelids as they fluttered shut. "I just want the rest of you."

"Cody."

"I know, I know, no serious talk." He released her. "We'll discuss that when I get back." He picked up his briefcase and the one suitcase he had thrown some clothes in last night after they had returned from the amusement park. "Oh, listen, could you maybe look in on Sean?"

She opened the door for him and then followed him into the hall. "Sure. Why? Is something wrong?" She remembered how warm Sean had felt when she had touched his forehead. "He did look a little tuckered out last night, but I thought it was because of the excitement."

"So did I, but he's running a slight fever this morning. I kept him home from school." Cody stopped by the exit. "Thelma's got him barricaded in bed with videotapes and comics."

"Sounds like a surefire cure to me." Lee reached up and smoothed down one side of his collar. "Don't worry, I'll look in on him."

He knew she would. "I appreciate it." He heard a short blast of a horn. The taxi, reminding him that the meter was running.

He was leaving. A queasy feeling was spilling out through her stomach. "I'm not doing it for you. I'm doing it for Sammy's number-one fan. I have some old Sammy tapes he might enjoy watching." She thought it over half a second, searching for something to keep her mind occupied so it wouldn't dwell on the sadness seeping in. "Heck, I might enjoy watching them, too.

I'll make an evening of it." She bit her lip as the taxi horn sounded again. "You be careful, you hear?"

He smiled, pleased with her concern. "It's not up to me to fly the plane."

She raised one eyebrow. "I do the funny lines here." Looking past Cody's shoulder, she saw Elyse waving to her. Time to get back to work.

"Lee?"

She looked up at Cody. "Yes?"

"I love you."

Lee's mouth dropped open. For a moment, her heart sprang up, savoring the words and hugging them to her as if they had texture, as if they were something she could actually touch and feel. Then she shook her head. "Don't say that, Cody."

Her response hurt. "I'm a grown man, Lee. No one tells me what I can or can't say. Or feel. See you in a week." He kissed her lips quickly and walked out.

Lee stared at the closed door. *Oh Cody, you don't know what you're asking of me.*

Lee hurried back down the hall to the soundstage, her body on automatic pilot. Her mind was on Cody. He had no right springing that on her, no right. He was making her dream all over again, even after she had promised herself to stop all this foolishness.

Sometimes, when she lay in bed at night, she could still hear Lloyd screaming at her, belittling her. She could still feel the humiliation, the hurt that had cut through her like a knife. She could still see the loathing in his eyes. She didn't want to see it in Cody's. The only way to make sure she never did was to go no further than she was right at this minute.

Lee hurried home from the studio after the taping session. She went straight to the file cabinet she housed in the garage and took out all her old tapes. Stuffing them into a canvas carryall, she threw the bag into the car and drove straight for Cody's house.

Thelma's face was pinched and drawn when she opened the door to admit Lee. Lee saw the concern immediately. "Hi, Thelma." She shut the door behind her. "How is he?"

Thelma wrung her thin hands together. She had never been any good in a crisis, even a minor one. "Oh, Miss Lee, I'm so glad you're here." She took the carryall from Lee as she pulled the younger woman toward the stairs. "He's getting worse. I was just about to call Mr. Lancaster and ask him what he wants me to do. Sean's rarely sick, and I've never had any children of my own, and—and—"

Lee placed a hand on the woman's shoulder to calm her. Thelma looked frightened and confused. "Why don't you let me see Sean, and then we'll decide whether to call Mr. Lancaster?"

There was no point in alarming Cody when he was a thousand miles away and couldn't do anything. It was probably just a bad cold.

When she walked into his room, Lee had to admit that Sean looked pretty miserable. She sat down on his bed and ran her hand through his hair. It was damp and plastered to his head. "Hi, Wolf. How's it going?"

Sean stirred a little, but the effort seemed to be too much for him. "I don't feel much like a wolf today, Lee."

She stroked his forehead. It felt very hot to the touch and his cheeks were flushed. There was a glazed look in his eyes. She didn't like it.

"You look like one sick cub to me," Sammy Squirrel told Sean.

He smiled weakly. "Maybe you can use your magic on me. I don't like being sick."

"Nobody likes being sick, sweetheart. But this takes something stronger than magic, I'm afraid." She reached for the thermometer Cody had left on the nightstand.

"Stronger than the Princess's magic?" Sean watched as she shook out the thermometer.

"'Fraid so. Open wide, honey." She tucked the slender rod under his tongue and held his hand. Thelma hovered over them, her clear blue eyes full of concern. "Does he have a pediatrician, Thelma?"

Thelma shook her head. "No, it was one of the things Mr. Lancaster said he was going to take care of as soon as he got back from his trip to Denver." Thelma looked at Sean, her brow furrowed. "Sean's always been so healthy."

Lee maintained a smile for Sean's benefit, but she was beginning to get worried. "He's not healthy now."

She waited for another three minutes, then took out the thermometer. The mercury registered between 104 and 105. She remembered reading somewhere that at 105 degrees a child could have convulsions. She wasn't about to wait around for that to happen.

"I'm going to take him to the walk-in clinic. It's only a couple of miles from here." Lee replaced the thermometer in its tube. "They should be able to get him in right away."

Thelma considered the situation. "But don't you have to be a parent or guardian to authorize treatment?" The slight, angular woman looked as if she was going to cry. "His mother took sick like this and then she—"

"Shh." Rising, Lee took hold of both the woman's hands and held them firmly. "You're not going to do him any good if you fall to pieces." Thelma nodded, obviously trying to get hold of herself for the boy's sake.

"But what are you going to do?" Thelma persisted.

Lee turned her attention to Sean. "Sean, by the power vested in me through Princess Enchantra, I've just become your mother for the afternoon. If anyone asks, I'm your mom. Okay?"

Sean barely nodded as he sank back into his pillow. His eyes closed and his breathing became labored. "I hurt, Lee."

"I know, honey, I know. But you'll be fine soon." Princess Enchantra added, "I promise."

"I'll get him dressed." Thelma hurried over to the closet.

Lee shook her head. She wanted to disturb the boy as little as possible. "I'll just take him the way he is. I can wrap him up in a blanket." As she spoke, she tucked the blanket around Sean. When she lifted him into her arms, he moaned. "I'm going to take you to the doctor, Sean. He'll give you some medicine that'll fix you right up." At least, she fervently hoped so.

Thelma stepped back to let Lee pass. "Will you need any help?"

"No, you stay here just in case Mr. Lancaster calls." Lee took the stairs cautiously, careful not to jar Sean any more than she had to. "He's bound to be worried if no one answers the phone."

Thelma hurried down the stairs just in front of Lee and opened the front door for her. "But shouldn't we call and tell him?"

"What can he do a thousand miles away?" Lee knew how she'd feel if it was her son and she was in Denver. Thoroughly helpless. "We'll let him know after we talk to the doctor."

The doctor on duty at the clinic had no reason not to believe Lee when she told him that she was Sean's mother. Since its purpose was to offer immediate, temporary care, the nurses at the clinic didn't bother working up any long histories on the people who sought their services. Lee knew enough about Sean to tell them that he had no known allergies as far as medication went and that he had had all his proper vaccinations. She had just talked about that with Cody last week. Sean had needed papers filled out for school and she had volunteered to help Cody do it.

Though they had waved her in ahead of several adults in the waiting room because of Sean's age and distress, Lee felt as if she were waiting an eternity before she saw the doctor. The doctor examined Sean, who was whimpering softly in Lee's arms, and ordered a chest X ray.

Forty-five minutes later, Sean was diagnosed as having walking pneumonia.

"Will he have to go to the hospital?" Lee asked. Sean looked at her, terrified. She held him tighter against her, rocking slightly.

"No, this medication should do the trick. No use scaring the poor little guy to death. I'm going to give him an injection to help reduce his fever. Then have this filled at our pharmacy." The doctor handed her two separate sheets. "Call if he doesn't improve."

Using one hand, Lee tucked the prescriptions into her purse. She kept a firm hold on Sean with the other.

When the nurse walked in with the injection, Sean began to cry.

"That's all right," Lee soothed. "Even soldiers cry."

Sean winced, holding on to her arm so tightly she thought the circulation was being cut off. "Really?"

"Princess's honor," Lee swore. The nurse gave her an odd look before she left the room.

Worn-out, Sean slept in the car on the way back. Thelma looked two shades paler as she threw open the door. It was obvious that the housekeeper had been waiting and watching at the window for their return.

"How is he?" she asked as she closed the door.

"He's going to be all right." Lee carried the sleeping Sean up the stairs and into his room. "How about you?"

"Me?"

Lee glanced over her shoulder just before she placed Sean on his bed. "You look like you're about to hyperventilate on me."

Thelma rushed over and pulled back the covers on the bed. "No, Miss Lee, I shan't."

Lee grinned wearily at the very proper, very British way that sounded. "See that you 'shan't.'" She pulled the comforter over Sean, then rubbed the sore spot on her back. "Think you can make us both some tea, Thelma?"

"Tea?" Thelma echoed, still looking at Sean.

She wanted Thelma kept occupied. "Yes, water, tea bags, lemon. Remember?" Lee took the medication from her purse and set it up on the nightstand.

Thelma came to. "Oh. Oh! Yes, of course." She began backing away.

Lee turned and smiled at her. "I'd appreciate it."

Thelma cast one last worried look at Sean. "And he'll—"

"Be all right, yes. I'll tell you everything over tea." Lee let out a long sigh as the woman left the room. "Gave us quite a scare, Sean," she murmured to the sleeping boy. "But it's going to be fine now."

Lee stayed and nursed Sean for the remainder of the day and created things for Thelma to do to keep the woman busy. She only left Sean's side long enough to go home and bring Pussycat back with her. She had no idea how long she was going to have to stay, and she didn't want to travel back and forth to feed the dog. Besides, it was nice to have the dog around to keep vigil with her.

Because Lee was there, when the phone rang that evening, it was a more subdued Thelma who answered.

"Oh, Mr. Lancaster," she cried happily as soon as Cody said her name. "He's going to be fine."

"Sean?" Why was she assuring him with such zeal? The boy just had a cold. Didn't he?

"Yes," Thelma continued in a rush. "The doctor said it was walking pneumonia, but—"

"What doctor?" Panic seized him. Pneumonia had been what Deborah had died of. How could this be happening again?

"The doctor at the clinic, he—"

Cody jumped up from his chair, dragging his suitcase onto the bed. The phone crashed to the floor as he reached for his clothes and tossed them in. He yanked it up from the floor. "Thelma, are you still there?"

"Yes, sir, but—"

"I'll be on the next plane back." Clothes spilled out of the suitcase. He left them where they fell. "Get him to a hospital right away and—"

"Mr. Lancaster, wait," Thelma pleaded. "The doctor doesn't think he has to go to one. Miss Lee is with Sean right now and—"

"Lee? Lee's with him?" He tried to get a grip on his rampaging emotions.

"Yes, sir. She took Sean to the clinic to see the doctor early this afternoon."

This afternoon? It was eight o'clock now. "Why didn't you call me right away?"

"Miss Lee said not to bother you. That you'd only worry."

She was right about that, he thought, dragging a hand through his hair. "How could she take him to a doctor? They won't treat Sean on her say-so." He paced, trying to organize his thoughts. "She's not his guardian."

"No, sir, but she told them she was Sean's mother."

His mother. The statement had him jarring to a halt. Maybe she would be, sooner than she thought. "Can you put her on?"

Thelma hesitated. "I think I saw her dozing off, sir, and she'd been through so much today that—"

"Never mind." Knowing Lee, she'd probably try to talk him out of returning. But he had to see Sean for himself before his fears could be laid to rest. "Just tell her that I'm taking the next flight out, Thelma."

"She's doing all she can, sir. She didn't want you to be worried."

The laugh he uttered was dry. "She has no say in the matter."

And neither, apparently, did he. All flights out of Denver's Stapleton International Airport were canceled as of that afternoon because of the snowstorm that had hit the city. Cody paced restlessly around the airport, trying to badger someone into flying out. But it was impossible. No flights were scheduled out until at least early next morning. Perhaps longer, a woman at a ticket counter informed him sympathetically.

If he took a turn for the worse, his son could be dead by early morning, he thought. Cody fought not to let panic get the better of him.

He stayed overnight in the airport, grabbing snatches of sleep in a chair that grew more torturous by the hour. He listened to every announcement over the loudspeaker, hoping to hear of a change. There was none.

The inclement weather continued into the next morning. More flights were cancelled. The airport grew steadily more crowded. And his panic attained a life of its own, feeding on demons of its own creation.

The phone lines were down and he couldn't call home to check on Sean. Cody's imagination tortured him. Life could go so quickly. Deborah had been fine one day, complaining of troubled breathing and an annoying cold the next. It lingered, but she refused to be alarmed. By the time she had agreed to see a doctor in the emergency room, it was too late. She was dead four hours after she walked into the admitting area.

That couldn't happen again. It couldn't. It wouldn't be fair.

But Cody knew that life wasn't fair.

When the phones became operable later in the afternoon, there were long lines to wait in. Everyone, it seemed, had someone to call. Cody waited impatiently. As he finally reached a phone, an announcement came over the loudspeaker that a flight to LAX was available and would be boarding shortly. He gave up his place in line and ran to the ticket counter. Cody got the last available seat.

When his taxi pulled up in front of his house at ten that evening, Cody saw that Lee's car was still in the driveway. He told himself that it was a good omen. He didn't know why, but it was. Having her here, having her magic here, made everything all right. He refused to think otherwise. He gave the driver a fistful of bills, knowing that it was more than the ride cost and not caring.

With his heart in his throat, Cody entered the house, tossing his bags by the door. He didn't even remember, once he was on the stairs, if he had closed the front door. All that mattered was seeing Sean home and in his bed, mending.

Taking the stairs two at a time, Cody hurried up the steps to Sean's room. The curtains at the window were opened, letting in the moonlight. Sean was in bed, asleep, his breathing steady. Cody let out the breath he had been holding. He looked over toward the window where Lee sat, her head resting on her arm. She seemed to be asleep as well.

Cody entered the room quietly. He didn't want to wake either of them, especially not Sean. But he needed to reassure himself that the boy was all right. All those hours he had been trapped at the airport, unable to reach them, waiting impatiently for the storm to be over and for a flight out, all he could think of over and over again was that Deborah had died of pneumonia. He had no idea what he would have done if he had lost Sean, too.

Ever so lightly, he stretched out his hand and touched the tips of his fingers to the small forehead. It was damp, but it felt cool. Sean stirred slightly beneath his touch, murmuring something in his sleep.

"The fever's gone."

Cody turned to see Lee watching him from her chair.

"I didn't mean to wake you," he whispered.

"I don't sleep too well in chairs. One of my strange habits. Welcome home." Lee rose and stretched before crossing to him. Every muscle in her body felt cramped and drained. She had hardly slept. She had kept vigil over Sean for Cody and for herself.

"C'mon." She took his arm and pulled him toward the hall. "I'll answer all your questions for you in the kitchen." She blinked as she walked out into the brightly lit hallway, then turned to Cody. "You look like hell."

He laughed softly, running a hand through her hair. It was tousled about her head. "I could return the compliment."

She lifted one shoulder in a half shrug as they went down the stairs. "I haven't slept very much in the last two days."

"Neither have I." He looked over his shoulder at the landing and the room beyond. "Is he going to be all right?"

Lee nodded, instinctively patting Cody's arm. "The worst is over. Fever broke this morning. He was more talkative tonight. He'll probably be restless by tomorrow. I suggest you play the videos for him that I brought over. By the way, I called in sick at the studio. The producer isn't very happy with me."

"Oh?" She had cared that much. Now that the crisis appeared to be over, Cody took another look at the situation. She had stayed with Sean, nursed him, giving up her own sleep to take care of the boy. No matter what she said to the contrary, she did at least love Sean. "I'll handle the producer."

"My hero." She stifled a large yawn as she followed him.

He walked into the kitchen and turned on the tap water. He could do with some more coffee. He'd been running on nothing but caffeine for the last eight hours. "You didn't have to do this, you know."

Using her hands for support against the table, Lee lowered herself onto a chair. "Sure I did. I couldn't just go home and leave him like this. He was running a high fever, and Thelma looked as if she was going to have a heart attack any second if I left her alone. I have to tell you, the woman makes terrific sandwiches, but she's not much in a crisis."

He took out the instant coffee and placed it on the counter, waiting for the water to boil. "And you are." It wasn't a question.

"Hey," she shrugged, "you cause enough of them, you learn how to deal with them as well."

As she sat and watched Cody, Lee leaned back in her chair. Her eyes felt heavy. Just for a moment, she told herself. She'd just close her eyes for one little moment.

When Cody turned around again, the two mugs in his hand, Lee had her head pillowed in her arms on the table. She was asleep. He set aside the coffee mugs and slipped an arm beneath either side of her body.

Lee opened her eyes as she felt herself being lifted. "I'm fine," she murmured. She made one quickly aborted effort to leave the shelter of his arms.

"You're exhausted," he corrected.

"That, too."

She felt light in his arms. "I'll take you to bed."

"I never argue with a man who has his arms full." She fought to keep her eyes open, but lack of sleep had caught up to her with a vengeance. She leaned her head against his chest as Cody carried her up the stairs. "This is nice, Cody."

"I was just thinking the same thing." He came to the landing. "Maybe we can do something about doing this on a more permanent basis."

But when he looked down at her face, he saw that she had fallen asleep. He shook his head. "Someday, Leanne," he said as he entered the guest room, "we are going to have this conversation where you can't run off or fall asleep."

He felt a wave of both love and gratitude wash over him. Cody kissed the top of her head lightly and then gently placed her on the bed. He drew the comforter over her and quietly closed the door behind him.

Suddenly feeling thoroughly drained, Cody went to his own room. He told himself that he needed to stretch out for just a few minutes.

He was asleep before his head hit the pillow.

Chapter Eleven

Lee woke up the next morning to the sound of laughter. It aroused a smile from her even as she was reorienting herself to her surroundings. She sat up and ran her fingers through her hair, then gave up. She needed to get her hands on a brush, and soon.

Rubbing her eyes, she stretched and stood up, then went to Sean's room. Cody was sitting on his son's bed. Pussycat was guarding both of them, his muzzle next to Sean's feet. It made for a nice scene, she thought. It stirred a yearning within her.

Three sets of eyes, two human, looked her way as she walked in. "Good morning, Sean. How do you feel?" To satisfy herself, she touched her lips to his forehead. It felt wonderfully cool.

Sean gave it some thought. "I feel kinda wobbly, but I'm not hot anymore. Can you play with me?" he asked hopefully.

"Sean," Cody said gently, "I don't think Lee wants to play right now."

No, she didn't. She wanted a hot shower and breakfast, but the disappointed look on Sean's face won her over. Lee dragged another hand through her hair. The brush would have to wait.

"Says who?" she asked Cody. She crossed to the games Sean kept neatly stacked on his shelves. There was one in particular that she knew he liked. "Are you up to this one?" She held it up for his inspection.

Sean pulled himself up into a sitting position. "Oh boy, am I."

"You're overruled." She made a smug face at Cody as she crossed back to Sean's bed.

Cody kissed her temple and saw Sean grinning broadly. "And you are incredible."

"I already know that," she quipped, making herself comfortable on the corner of the bed.

No, I don't really think you do, Cody thought. "I'm going to take a quick shower. Call me if you need me."

That's the trouble, she thought. *I think I already do.* Lee rolled up her sleeves. "Prepare to lose, earth scum," she warned Sean in a voice she used to depict evil villains.

Cody shook his head as he walked out. There was absolutely no way he was letting this woman escape from his life.

Cody walked her to her car later that evening and held the door open for her. Pussycat jumped in first, making himself comfortable in the back seat.

"Are you sure you don't want to stay?" Cody nodded toward the back seat and Pussycat. "You're practically all moved in already."

"You're forgetting all my junk at home," she teased evasively. There was nothing more she wanted to do than to give herself to this man, to move in and live happily ever after.

Except that she knew it couldn't be done.

Leaning in through the rolled-down car window, Cody took her hand in his. "I'm remembering the only important thing. You." He saw the same wary look entering her eyes and he bit back his impatience. "We still need to have that talk, you know."

"Later." It was meant to be a light remark. It came out like a plea. She didn't want things to end between them, not yet, and they would. If he pressed her, they would. She couldn't overcome the fears, the memories that haunted the chambers of her mind. Perhaps in time, but not yet.

"Later," he agreed, stepping back and letting her go. *But not too much later.*

Cody stood there as she backed out of the driveway and onto the street. He waved and stood there for a long while after she had disappeared from sight.

The rest of the week, while Sean was convalescing, Lee managed to find time each day to come over and entertain him. Cody quickly grew used to finding her there each evening when he arrived home, used to seeing her across the table from him at dinner with Sean between them. It was something he wanted on a permanent basis. He didn't like the feeling of wondering if she would be with them the next night. He wanted to be certain.

Though he struggled to maintain his patience, he had reached the point that they were going to have to sit down and have a long discussion. He would have been lying if he pretended not to be afraid of the outcome. But he couldn't go on like this. It was time to have things out between them once and for all, to put things in the past to rest and finally go on with their lives.

Lee stayed late on Friday. The weekend before her, there was no reason to hurry home. With the television screen taken over by a video game, Cody bided his time, watching Lee and Sean play one continuous game for two and a half hours. Finally, worn-out, Sean had surrendered his control to Lee and offered to watch her play alone. He fell asleep shortly thereafter.

Cody carried him upstairs, and they both put the boy to bed.

"Looks like an angel, doesn't he?" she murmured.

"He's a healthy, happy boy again, thanks to you," Cody replied. He moved to put his arm around her, but she had already stepped into the hallway,

Lee shrugged off the compliment. "It would have happened, anyway, sooner or later," she told him as she walked down the stairs. "You're a good father." Looking around the living room, she saw her purse on the sofa and crossed to it. "Well, I'd better be—"

Cody put his hand on her purse. "I'd like you to stay, Lee."

Lee looked into Cody's eyes. Here it was, she thought, the showdown. She looked toward the door. "I'm really kind of tired, Cody."

His hand remained where it was. "Stay."

"You do have a way with words." Reluctantly, she let go of her purse and sat on the sofa, fighting tension. "Is that anything like 'heel'?"

Cody sat next to her, searching for the right words. "I want to talk. About us."

She didn't want to go through what she knew was coming. "What about us?"

"That's exactly it, there is no 'us,' not until you tell me what I need to know." He placed his hands on her shoulders, as if to anchor her attention. She realized he had taken his wedding ring off. Her stomach tightened. "Lee, I want to know."

She sought refuge behind her humor, although she knew that this time it wasn't going to work. "Thirst for knowledge is a very admirable thing. The encyclopedia would be a good place to start."

He held on to his temper, though it was wearing thin. "Lee, I want to know about your first marriage."

She didn't want to talk about it, to admit that she had let it happen. "Why?"

He tried hard to be gentle with her, but it wasn't easy, not anymore. "Because until I do, we're not going to get any further in our relationship."

She raised her chin defensively, her last barrier crumbling. "Maybe I don't want to go any further."

"I think you do."

She looked away, not knowing what to say, how to answer. She did want it to go on, but oh, at what price?

Cody felt his temper slipping. He felt like shaking her, making her tell him. He could only ask. And hope. "Please, Lee."

She closed her eyes for a moment. "You certainly know how to unravel me."

"I've been taking notes."

A sad smile played on her lips. Maybe she did owe him an explanation. He deserved to know why she couldn't open her heart to him, why loving him, laying herself bare to him, would be the worst thing in the world for her.

"All right. I'll tell you." She rose, unable to sit still while she talked. Her own words agitated her even as they burned inside. "All my life I wanted a home, a family, people to love who loved me back. A person to love." She said the words softly, as if to herself. "It didn't quite work out with my parents. I was confident I could do better on my own. I left my father's house and went off to college. The first semester I met Lloyd. I was eighteen."

Lee crossed to the window and looked out. It was pitch-black outside, just the way it was within her soul. "I can still remember the first day I saw him. He was tall, with thick, sandy blond hair, and he had this incredible, wide smile. And he was smiling at me. At me," she repeated, emphasizing the effect.

She turned to look at Cody for a moment, a half smile on her face. "I thought he was everything I was looking for. We started dating. He told me he loved me on our second date. I thought he meant it, and I was in heaven. He was so beautiful. At least, on the outside." She looked away, remembering. It caused her physical pain to remember.

"Inside, he wasn't so beautiful. But I didn't see that, not at first. I just saw someone who told me he loved me, someone who wanted me in his life. Forever." The word had such a hollow ring to it now. "We got married. After a while, a very short while, everything I did started to annoy him."

Cody found himself hating the man. He wanted to interrupt, to tell her that Lloyd hadn't been worthy of her love. But he had to hear her out. If he said anything, he was afraid that she wouldn't go on.

Lee began to pace the room slowly as the thoughts poured from her. "I couldn't do anything to please him.

And I tried. Oh God, I tried so very hard. I dropped out of school. We couldn't both go to college. Someone had to earn a living, and his education was more important—at least, that's what he made me believe. He was going to be a lawyer. Then he switched majors when he started flunking courses. It went on like that for about a year, switching and flunking. Finally, he dropped out altogether. He told me it was my fault. He couldn't study, worrying about money.'' A disparaging smile flittered over her lips. ''I didn't earn enough.''

Lee tried to keep the bitterness at bay, but it broke through. ''I got a second job. Things got worse. He'd do something like smash the car up—well, these things happened, he'd say. I'd burn the toast, and it made the evening news. He'd yell, telling me how stupid I was.''

Cody couldn't remain quiet any longer. ''Why didn't you leave him?''

It hadn't been that simple for her. ''Because I kept hoping it would change, that he would change. That somehow, magically, I'd pull it all together and he'd love me.'' There were tears shining in her eyes now. Tears for the fool she had been to hope. ''That was the way it was supposed to be. Except it wasn't.'' Without realizing it, she ran her hand along her cheek. She could still feel it, the blow that had ended it all.

And then Cody knew. ''He hit you?'' He clenched his fists at his sides.

''Just once. That was when I gave up and left.'' She turned then to look at him. ''But I had put up with all the things that came before. I let it all happen. I let him use me. I traded the last of my self-esteem for love. It's taken me a long time to work my way back.''

Cody didn't know how to break down her walls. ''I'm not Lloyd.''

She moved away, out of reach. She needed to be able to think. She couldn't think when he touched her. "No, but don't you see? If it doesn't work out with you, then there are no dreams left. I'd rather hope somewhere in my heart and not know, than know it can't be and have no hope left at all."

She fought the urge to fall into his arms, to make him promise that things wouldn't be that way. But that would have been weak, and more than anything else, she had to stay strong. It was all she had. "Why can't you just let things continue the way they have been?" She backed away from Cody.

But he was quicker and took hold of her by the shoulders. "Because I don't want to risk having you drift out of my life, Lee. I'm tired of shadowboxing with some ghost from the past, wondering if I did or said something to remind you of him. I'm *not* him," he insisted, "I'm me."

"I know that," she cried. "Intellectually, I know that. In my heart, I know that. But there's this other dimension—"

He couldn't help the sarcasm that came into his voice. He didn't want to be judged by someone else's failures. "Oh, we're into time travel now."

She licked her lips. "Princess Enchantra—"

"I don't give a damn about Princess Enchantra! I care about you. Just you."

It was happening again, coming apart, just as it had the last time. She jerked away from him, wincing. "Don't yell at me."

"I'll yell if I want to!" But then he lowered his voice, not wanting to wake Sean, not wanting to bring Thelma into this. "Yelling is healthy. Don't cringe, dammit. I'm not going to hit you." He was so frustrated, he wanted to lash out at something. "I wish he was here so I could hit him, but not you. Don't you get it yet? I love you." Why couldn't she get that through her thick head?

"Yes, I know." But she had heard those words once before, believed in those words once before, and paid the price.

"And you love me." It wasn't a question. He knew.

Lee looked away. Cupping her chin in his hand, he forced her to look up at him. "And you love me."

"Yes." There was no use in lying.

Where should he go from here? "So?"

She pulled away again. Why didn't he understand how hard it was for her to trust someone again? "I'm scared, Cody. I need time."

He shoved his hands in his pockets. "How much time?"

"I don't know. A long time."

He knew he couldn't force her. He had seen what a quick flash of his temper had done. It would only serve to push her farther away. But, God, it was so hard to be patient when he wanted her so badly.

Cody dug deep for one touch of humor. It was the only thing she seemed to respond to. "Don't wait too long, Lee. I might forget what to do on our honeymoon."

She smiled and touched his face. She wished she could get over her demons, wished it with all her heart. "I'd remind you."

He caught her hand in his and turned it palm up. The soft kiss he pressed there sent a shiver coursing up her spine.

"I'd better go." She turned from him.

"Lee?"

Lee looked back at him, not knowing what else there was left to be said. "Yes?"

"One more thing. I'd like you to sleep on this." With no warning but the look in his eyes, Cody pulled her into his arms and kissed her. There were fewer explosions at the bicentennial birthday celebration of the Declaration of Independence. Knowing what to expect and yet not knowing, her entire body softened, molding against his as she was swept away with bombs bursting in air.

Each time he kissed her, it nullified her mind, reduced her sensibilities to rubble and made her forget every promise she had made to herself.

Pulses throbbed, rushing noises overcame her powers of hearing, and she heard, sensed, tasted, felt and saw nothing but Cody.

When he stopped kissing her, there was a wicked look in his eyes he struggled hard to maintain.

There was no point in pretending that she could breathe normally. "You expect me—" she pulled in air "—to sleep after that?"

Even when he felt like throttling her, she made him want to laugh. "No, I expect you to come around after that."

"I'll try," she promised. "I'll really, really try."

Lee drove home in a fog, struggling vainly with her worst fears and trying to put them to rest. She was in a total state of confusion when she unlocked her front door and walked in. Something was standing right in her way and she nearly tripped over it.

"What the—?"

Feeling around for the light switch, she turned it on and then she saw it. The Sammy Squirrel stuffed animal she had given Sean was back. It was standing in the middle of the living room with a bouquet of violets tied to its hands.

Pinned to its tail was a note that read: Marry me.

Pussycat padded in from the kitchen, gave the squirrel a disinterested sniff and barked at Lee. She looked at him, the note in her hand. "And where were you while Cody was breaking in?"

Apparently unwilling to go through an interrogation, Pussycat withdrew to the kitchen.

Lee pulled the stuffed animal over to one side, planted herself on the sofa and tapped out Cody's number on the telephone. A resonant voice answered on the first ring.

He'd been waiting for her, she thought.

Lee fingered the note. "I take it that Sammy is not speaking for himself."

Cody had smuggled the stuffed animal into her house before he had come home. Since he had made up his mind to confront her about her ex-husband that evening, he had thought the air would be cleared. He hadn't thought things would end the way they had.

Now that he had laid himself on the line, was she going to turn him down? "He told me you weren't his type. No tail."

She let the note drop to the coffee table. "How did you get in?"

"I used to be a second-story man."

"At six-two that's hardly likely."

"All right, Pussycat let me in." Actually, he had made his own way in. She had left a back window unlocked. He'd made sure the house was secure before he'd left.

Lee laughed softly. "Knew he couldn't be trusted."

"I like him just fine, except for his name."

They were waltzing around the inevitable, she thought helplessly. It was best if she put a stop to it now. "Cody, you're rushing me."

He didn't want to hear her say no. "Lee, I saw you with Sean. I've held you in my arms. I'm not reading things into this. We belong together."

She dragged her hand through her hair. "We *are* together."

"*Married* together."

She closed her eyes, sinking farther into the sofa. Why, oh why couldn't she stop being afraid? He was a good man. "It's a big step and there's no net."

"You don't need a net. I'll be there to catch you, Lee. You won't fall."

She should just say no and be done with it. But she couldn't form the word. As afraid as she was of disappointment, of having her dreams shattered, she couldn't do the same to him, couldn't hurt him. "Let me think about it."

"So we're back to a holding pattern," he murmured.

"I'm sorry, Cody, I don't want to put you through this. Maybe I should—"

But he wouldn't give her a chance to turn him down. "Get a good night's sleep. I'll tell you what, I'll give you the weekend to figure out how terrific I am. We'll talk on Monday."

She sighed. Maybe she *should* have her head examined. "Thanks for being so understanding, Cody."

"Don't mention it."

Lee hung up and then looked at the squirrel. The bouquet was still in its hands. She leaned over and removed it, then inhaled the fragrance. "What do you think, Pussycat? Think I'm crazy?"

The dog looked at her with huge, accusing eyes as he reentered the room.

"You would. He bought you off with cookies." And he had bought her off with kisses of fire that singed her soul.

Oh God, what was she going to do? She closed her eyes as the memories flooded back. It wasn't fair to judge Cody against what Lloyd had done, yet she couldn't rid herself of the fear that it would happen again. Somehow, some way, it might happen again. And this time, she might not be able to pull herself together again. This time, all that she was would disintegrate.

She sat on the sofa for a long time just staring at the note on the coffee table.

Chapter Twelve

Cody slowly replaced the telephone receiver into the cradle. She was going to turn him down. If not now, later. He had heard it in her voice. By not letting her say it now, he was just postponing the inevitable. Maybe it wasn't meant to be.

No, dammit. She *did* love him. She'd admitted it. She was like a swimmer, trapped under ice. He could see her but he couldn't reach her. Somewhere, a crack in the ice existed and he was going to find it and free her. Free them both.

Cody dragged his hands through his hair and sighed. There wasn't anything he could do tonight. He'd given it his best shot. Maybe tomorrow something he hadn't already thought of would suggest itself. He pushed himself from the sofa, feeling drained and tired. Cody went upstairs and checked on Sean before he went to bed.

Sean was awake. He sat up when his father looked in. "Did she find Sammy?" he asked eagerly. His father had asked to "borrow" Sammy, and Sean had been excited when Cody explained why he needed the stuffed animal. Sean wanted Lee to live with them forever. He missed his mom a lot, and though Lee was a lot funnier than his mom had been, she held him like a mom and he liked that.

"Yes," Cody said. "She found him."

Sean didn't understand the look on his father's face. Why was it so sad? "And she said yes, right?"

"No, she didn't." Even in his frustration, Cody still took comfort from the newly reformed relationship he had with Sean. He dropped down on the bed, sitting next to Sean.

Sean tried hard to understand. "How come?"

"She says she needs some time."

"For what?" Sean tilted his head. It just didn't make sense to him. "She likes us."

There was no question about it in the young boy's voice. Oh, to be filled with that much confidence and conviction again. "Yes." Cody smiled. "She likes us."

Obviously, his dad and Lee were making this too hard. Grown-ups always did. "Then it's a piece of cake."

"It should be." Cody tucked Sean in. "It should be." He rose. "You get some sleep, hear?"

Sean nodded and watched his father leave the room. But even after the lights went out, Sean didn't close his eyes. He had a lot of thinking to do.

Cody liked to stay in bed an extra hour on Saturday. It was the only day of the week he allowed himself to sleep in and relax. But this morning he felt the need to go out and run. He wanted to clear his head a little, to put things into perspective. A lot had happened in his life in a very short time.

Most of the neighborhood was still asleep. Only one car passed by as he made his way up and then down the long winding path that led through the development. He had only scrub jays for companions, and their noisy screeching faded into the background as he felt his blood pumping and he absorbed the continual rhythm of his feet meeting the pavement.

An elderly walker, dressed in a white sweat suit, passed him going in the opposite direction. He nodded his head, his eyes held firm in concentration. Cody uttered a preoccupied "'Morning," as he continued on his way. Sweat was swirling down along his spine and across his forehead. His pace was more intense than normal. Cody slowed down.

Maybe he was rushing things with Lee, too, just as she had said. He'd take it easy, he promised himself, dragging air back into his lungs. Let things evolve naturally. Just because it had turned out to be so easy for him didn't necessarily mean that she could jump into a relationship—a marriage—quickly.

Some women needed time. Even whirling dervishes. And when she finally realized just how much love she was turning her back on, he'd be there for her.

Satisfied, Cody turned for home.

The hot water from the shower felt good as it pulsated along his tight muscles. He'd have breakfast with Sean, Cody decided, drying himself off. Just the two of them, and they'd plan a day without Lee. It could still be done.

Cody drew on a pair of jeans and then tugged on his favorite gray pullover. It took time now to come up with things to do without Lee. Funny how quickly she had become an integral part of their lives with absolutely no effort on her part.

After passing a comb through his wet hair, Cody swung by Sean's room. "Hey, Sean, what do you say to a little breakfast?" Cody looked in, but Sean was nowhere in the room. The bed was empty. Odd. He usually had to be blasted out of bed. "Sean?" Cody walked in and looked around. The bathroom door was open. "Where are you?"

There was a small crumpled heap of clothing on the floor next to the bed. Cody picked it up. Sean's pajamas. He probably just got tired of lying around in bed and went outside to play, Cody guessed, dropping the pajamas on the bed.

Cody turned to leave the room. Something crunched under his foot. He bent down and saw that he had stepped on a piece of Sean's bank.

It had been broken open.

Cody stared at the smashed bank. Why would Sean deliberately break it? He didn't need any money. If he wanted anything, all he had to do was ask. What was going on? And where was he?

"Thelma," Cody called, trying to keep the urgency he felt building out of his voice as he walked out into the hallway. "Thelma!"

The older woman came hurrying to the foot of the stairs. "Yes, Mr. Lancaster?"

"Where's Sean?"

She looked at Cody a little strangely. "Why, he's in bed, sir."

Cody walked down to join her. "No, he's not."

Thelma's forehead wrinkled in confusion. "Well then, where is he? He's not down here."

"I don't know." Cody began to walk toward the back door. Maybe Sean was in the yard. It was possible he

could have just slipped by Thelma while she was working. That still didn't explain why he had broken open his
bank, but maybe that had just been an accident. No,
Sean was a very neat, orderly little boy. He would have
put away his pajamas and cleaned up the mess. Unless
something was wrong.

Thelma followed quickly in his wake. They both
looked out on a wide open, empty yard. The scene was
duplicated in the front.

Lee had spent most of the night wide awake, tossing
around on her bed. She didn't like to think in the night.
Nighttime was when it was the worst, when the empti-
ness hurt and memories of the past rose up to haunt her,
to remind her of what had been and what had failed to
be.

But it was the time when she couldn't hide from herself, when she was the sternest with her feelings.

Somewhere around three o'clock, she had sat up, exhausted and frustrated. And thinking clearly for perhaps the first time in a long time. She turned on the
radio, pulled her knees up to her chin and thought it
through.

What was she running from? Commitment? She had
already committed to Cody, to Sean, and she knew it.
That left what—happiness and love for her to be running from? She needed those as much as she needed to
breathe. Marriage was something that she had always
wanted, had always believed in. She had dreamed about
it being her answer to everything. It wasn't an answer,
but it was a start, a point from which to grow, to blos-
som. With the right man.

That was what she had needed all along. The right
man. She knew people weren't all alike. Cody wasn't
anything like Lloyd, not on the inside. Though Lloyd

had been almost exquisitely handsome, he had turned out to be costume jewelry. Cody, with his rugged good looks, was gold. Solid. Lloyd had used her, and she was afraid that would happen again. But Cody only wanted to make her happy. He was a kind, loving man. She had seen evidence of that over and over again.

It was the past she was running from, and the mistakes that existed there. If she left them in the past, if she started fresh, it would be all right.

Letting out a breath, she switched off the radio again. She laid back and smiled and fell asleep.

When the buzzing noise penetrated her brain, Lee flung out her hand, dragging the canopy drape with it, and pushed on the button of her alarm clock. Why was it ringing? It was Saturday. She hadn't set it.

And why was it still ringing?

Lee sat up, rubbing the sleep from her eyes, trying to clear the cobwebs from her brain. The phone. The phone was ringing. She pulled it over to her bed. "Hello?"

"Lee." Cody's voice made her blink and then focus her thoughts. He sounded upset. "Is Sean there with you?"

"No." Why would Sean be here by himself? "Why?"

"Because he's not here. I can't find him."

"Slowly, Cody. I just woke up." She dragged her hand over her face and took a couple of deep breaths as she kicked off her covers. "What do you mean you can't find him?" Hurriedly, she reached for her robe and juggled the phone as she slipped it on.

"When I got back from running this morning, he wasn't in his room. He's not anywhere in the house, and Thelma hasn't seen him."

That wasn't like Sean. And he had barely gotten over being sick. Where would he go? "Maybe he's just over at a friend's house."

"He wouldn't go without telling me. Besides, I've already tried every number I could think of. He broke open his piggy bank before he left."

"That makes it sound as if he was running away." But he had seemed so happy last night before he had fallen asleep. "Did you have an argument with him?"

"No, and he wouldn't run away even if I had. He knows I'm harmless, even if you don't." The last part came out inadvertently.

She thought of the night she had just spent. "You're not as harmless as you think." She heard the doorbell ring several times in succession.

"Lee, I'm going to call the police. Call me if he should show up."

"Hang on," she urged. "The doorbell just rang. Maybe it's him." Lee placed the receiver down on her bed and ran to the door, fumbling with the sash on her robe. "Coming!" Please, please let that be Sean, she prayed. She didn't want to think about what could happen to a little boy wandering around alone.

She swung the door open and let out a huge sigh. Pussycat barked behind her, and the tall, burly man standing next to Sean looked over Lee's shoulder uneasily.

Lee dropped to her knees and threw her arms around Sean, pulling him close. "Oh, Sean, we've been so worried about you." She drew back, still on her knees, to look him over. He seemed all right. "Your dad's on the phone right now and—"

The burly man hung back on the front step, carefully watching Pussycat's every move. "Look, lady, don't mean to break up this happy reunion, but somebody still owes me fifteen dollars."

Lee rose, her hand on Sean's shoulder to keep him from moving. "Excuse me?"

The man jerked his thumb at the curb. Lee looked around his bulky frame and saw a taxicab parked there. "This little kid flagged me down. I picked him up a few miles away. He gave me your address. He only had three dollars and fifty-three cents on him. That doesn't begin to cover the fare, but he said you'd pay. I didn't want to leave him wandering around by himself, so I brought him here, but my supervisor—"

Lee held up a hand. "Say no more." Quickly, she went to get her purse from the hall closet. She returned to the doorway and handed the man a twenty.

He looked uncertainly at it. "Um, wait here. I've got—"

"Keep the change," she told him. The man broke out into a toothy grin. "And thanks for bringing him." She took Sean's hand and closed the door. "C'mon, we've got to tell your dad you're safe."

She hurried to the nearest phone and picked it up. "Cody, he's here."

"Sean?" It had taken her so long to get back to him, he was afraid to hope.

"Yes."

Cody let out a sigh of relief. Then anger set in. How could Sean have put him through all this? Hadn't he been through enough these last few days? "Hold him until I can get over there."

She hung up and gave Sean a long, searching look. "He sounds pretty angry, Sean."

Sean had forgotten how jumpy grown-ups were. But he had a mission and he had to carry it out. His dad would understand once he explained. "I didn't mean to make him angry."

"I know." Kids did things on impulse. She could remember several things that had earned her a severe tongue-lashing when she was young. She looked at Sean and saw that he seemed agitated himself. "Are you feeling all right?"

"Yeah. I'm not sick anymore," he told her proudly. He wondered if she remembered that he had cried in the doctor's office and if that would make her change her mind.

She cast about for a way to get him to tell her why he had run away. "That's good. You want a hot chocolate?"

"Sure." His throat was feeling a little dry, Sean thought. And she always used these neat marshmallows in her chocolate.

Lee took Sean's hand and led him to the kitchen. The dog followed faithfully. Sean felt better with Pussycat along. He'd never done this before, and even though he told his dad it was easy, maybe it wasn't.

"You know, you gave us an awful scare." She poured a cup of milk into a pot and turned on the flame. She could have easily slipped into Sammy Squirrel's voice, but this seemed too important for a cartoon character. She looked into Sean's deep green eyes. "Why did you run away from home, Sean?"

Sean stopped petting Pussycat and looked at her, confused. Where did she get that idea? "I didn't run away from home. I came to see you."

"Me?" She sank down in the chair next to him. "Why?"

He licked his lips, hoping this would work. "I want to ask you to marry me."

For a second, absolutely no sound came out of her mouth. Finally, she choked out one word. "What?"

"Well," Sean explained hurriedly, "Dad told me last night that he didn't think you were going to marry him, so I wanted to ask you before someone else did and you married him. This way, we can still have you in the family. Will you marry me, Lee?" He ran out of breath.

She brushed his hair away from his face, tears gathering in her eyes. And this was part of what she was running from? What was she, crazy? "That's the very nicest proposal I ever got."

He saw the tears in her eyes. Why was she crying? Didn't she like him? "So, will you?"

Just then, the stove started to hiss as the milk bubbled over, meeting the burner. She jumped up and pulled it off the stove, then dumped the whole thing into the sink. The hot chocolate could wait.

She turned and looked at Sean who was watching her with large eyes, waiting. She dropped down to her knees again and placed a hand on each of his small shoulders. "I'm afraid I'm a little too old for you, Sean." She saw his expression fall and knew she was falling in love twice over. What an idiot she had been for doubting. "So I'm going to have to settle for your dad."

The sad expression faded instantly as he brightened. "That's okay. He likes you almost as much as I do." Deciding that maybe he would have better luck at it than she did, Sean took the carton of milk out of the refrigerator and placed it on the counter. Lee started to take out another pot. "No, cold's okay, too."

She grinned at him. A very practical little boy she was getting, she thought. She poured a glass and mixed it for him, then turned her attention to the burned pot. She didn't want him to see her cry. Little boys didn't understand tears of happiness, and hers had been locked in-side for so long.

Sean took a long sip. "You know, he's been awfully sad since Mom went to the angels. You make him happy, just like you make me happy. You've made him a nicer dad, just like he used to be."

Lee dried her hands and sat down next to him again. She ruffled his hair. "Sean, you just made me an offer I can't refuse. I get two for the price of one."

"Huh?"

"Never mind." She laughed. "You'll understand when you grow up. And I intend to be there when you do." She couldn't wait to see Cody and tell him.

As if in answer to her thoughts, the doorbell rang. Lee sprang up instantly. "I guess your dad flew through some red lights to get here," she said over her shoulder to the boy and dog following her as she ran to the front door.

"Yes!" she cried as she threw open the door.

The impatience on Cody's face dissolved to confu-sion. "Yes, what?"

Lee wanted to cry, laugh, everything at once. She settled for flinging her arms around Cody's neck. "Yes, I'll marry both of you."

He looked over Lee's shoulder and saw Sean. His son had a very self-satisfied smile on his face. "What did you do?"

"I asked her to marry us. See, Dad, I told you it was a piece of cake. She just needed the right guy to ask her, that's all."

"Yes," Lee whispered to Cody, "I guess I did. The offer still open?"

He still wasn't sure what had just happened, but he didn't care. He tightened his arms around her. "The offer never closed."

Why hadn't she realized before how very good, how very safe, she felt in his arms? "That's good, because I did a lot of thinking last night after I hung up. I thought about leaving here. Leaving you." She saw his expression darken. "And then I realized that I'd be doing to myself exactly what I was afraid of having happen. I didn't want to get involved because I was afraid of being emotionally abandoned again. By leaving you, I'd be accomplishing the same thing." She laughed as she shook her head at her own stupidity. She had almost turned her back on what she had always wanted. "It's too late to run for cover. You've completely ruined me for a life of solitude, Cody Lancaster, and now you're going to have to pay the price."

"I guess I'll just have to marry you, then."

She nodded solemnly, biting her lower lip to keep from laughing again. "I guess so."

Sean looked on as his father kissed Lee, then grinned at the Sammy Squirrel doll Lee had left standing in the corner. He gave the stuffed animal a thumbs-up sign like the big kids did at school.

"We did it," Sean said to the squirrel.

And he could have sworn that the squirrel's toothy grin grew just a little broader. But then, Sean already knew that Lee's house was always full of magic. And never more than now.

* * * * *

**Three All-American beauties discover
love comes in all shapes and sizes!**

ALL-AMERICAN SWEETHEARTS

by Laurie Paige

CARA'S BELOVED (#917)—*February*
SALLY'S BEAU (#923)—*March*
VICTORIA'S CONQUEST (#933)—*April*

A lost love, a new love and a hidden one, three *All-American
Sweethearts* get their men in Paradise Falls, West Virginia.
Only in America... and only from Silhouette Romance!

Silhouette
ROMANCE™

Take 4 bestselling love stories FREE

Plus get a FREE surprise gift!

A romantic collection that
will touch your heart....

to Mother with Love '93

Diana Palmer
Debbie Macomber
Judith Duncan

As part of your annual tribute to
motherhood, join three of Silhouette's
best-loved authors as they celebrate the
joy of one of our most precious gifts—
mothers.

Available in May at your favorite retail outlet.

Only from ▼™ *Silhouette*®

—where passion lives.

SMD93